Rickshaw

Rickshaw

David McGrath

THISTLE
PUBLISHING

First published in 2015 by:

Thistle Publishing
36 Great Smith Street
London
SW1P 3BU

www.thistlepublishing.co.uk

ISBN-13: 978-1-910670-04-0

For Jo

STINK

I was a lout, a twenty-something young lad with no direction, waking horrified in a London doorway, a life left behind burnt to the ground.

I needed to sort something out.

Hangovers are when there is not enough water in the body to complete Krebs cycles. Such biology was for the smart kids in school. There was nothing in woodwork about Krebs cycles or eukaryotic cells or mitochondria. The *Alcoholism Explained* pamphlet taught me the whole lot.

I needed to sort something out.

It was my first time out of Ireland and I expected more, as though someone should have been handing out achievement certificates, not everybody sauntering about like it was normal.

'Ladies and Gentlemen,' a street performer shouted. He was in a straight jacket. I thought, you and me both, buddy. 'This is how I make my living, performing escape feats all around the world for lovely people such as yourselves. If you like what you see here today, please show your appreciation at the end with some coin. If you don't have money, that's fine, come up at the end and say *Thank You*. It's just as much appreciated. All right, here I go!'

I felt my hangover revving up behind my eyeballs like a bulldozer.

The street performer pressed play on his stereo with his big toe. A grainy music full of uncomfortable bass began. He started to wriggle and I started to feel my brain drip out of my ears just watching the prick. I decided to put off the bulldozer for another day. I would sort something out tomorrow. Humanity was doomed and we were all going to die—drink time.

London was a beast. The wealth of the world had poured into it for as long as the Brits had ruled the world and the buildings wanted everyone to know it—mansions and palaces with Rolls Royces parked out front, stained glass, marble, gold trimming. Red double decker buses were going places I had never heard of before. There was fine dining all over, doormen in fancy suits and top hats and chaps, lots of chaps and they said *Oh, well done* to other chaps. A lot of Irish guys had a grievance with the English. I didn't. I admired those men in the easy chairs who smoked pipes and carved up the world for centuries, constantly setting the rules so that they won every time.

Even conversation on the street was different to Ireland. 'The people I nanny for,' one woman said to her friend, 'think that my name is too posh for a servant so they've said they're calling me Lucy from now on.'

Seventeen-year-old young lads flew by in Lamborghini Murcielagos. Those things were the price of houses and the kids in them had hurt expressions as though they had asked for a Bugatti Veyron and all they got was a shitty Murcielago.

One thing London had going for it—stealing was easy. I picked up booze and walked out the shop door with it as though I owned the place, right in front of the staff and security. They were all so dazed by long hours and minimum wage that I could have stolen their shoes without them noticing.

'You're nicked,' a voice said from behind me as I carried a crate of beer out a front door. I was happy, like I was being taken off my own hands, like I was someone else's problem now.

I was disappointed to face a junkie when I turned. The junkies in Dublin had the same sharp look, the same gaunt frame. A bulging sports bag hung by a strap from his shoulder. He looked at me with sharp, glassy eyes then moved closer so that only my crate of beer was between our chests. His smell was in his breath and off his clothes, wafting up from him like it was throwing a punch.

'It is a pleasant day. A crisp breeze. A shining sun. Shall we frequent the park to drink your libations?' he said. And with that, on he shuffled, his eye not on me anymore but on the street and the people in it.

I followed him to the National Gallery when he spotted a group of Chinese tourists on their way inside. He came between the first of them and the door then produced a book of raffle tickets from his hoodie.

'How many is in your party?' he said.

'Twenty-six,' a Chinese lady said.

'I will only charge you for twenty.'

'Free?' she asked, confused, searching for her guide book. 'Free?'

'Out of date information,' the junkie said. 'Information no good.'

'How much?' the lady asked.

'Five pounds each is a hundred pounds, Madam,' he said, tearing away twenty-six raffle tickets from the book and handing them to her. 'Would you care to pay the entire amount and fix up with your party later? Just that it's busy and I *am* doing you a favour.'

The lady was twenty pounds short. Her husband took out his wallet and made the hundred.

'Thank you, folks,' he said. 'Enjoy.'

The lady handed out the raffle tickets to the rest of the group.

The junkie jogged on.

'That was brilliant,' I said on catching up.

'Your notion of brilliance is misaligned, Irish,' he said. He was the first person to call me Irish.

'What's your name?'

'Stink,' he said.

Stink pulled the same trick outside Ripley's on Piccadilly Circus and the Royal Academy of Art. His walk was a hunt. He handed out directions for pound coins and collected money in the crowd for street performers during their performance, the street performer completely unaware he was doing it.

'Show your appreciation, folks,' he said and the people gave him money just to get him away from them. He plucked lights from bicycles like they were ripened fruit and shoved them into his hoodie along with handfuls of postcards he grabbed off the racks outside newsagents. Anything not nailed down was fair game.

We entered a park, picked a bench in front of a lake and cracked open a bottle of beer each. Stink sank his in one then cracked open another.

We were there a while, saying nothing much when a man approached, a respectable type in a cardigan. He stopped beside us, looked around then said, 'You get the books?'

'In the bag,' Stink said.

'All of them?'

'I couldn't get the Mayan one. Out of print apparently.'

'I need that one.'

'We all need something.'

The man picked up the bag, threw Stink a fifty then was off. Stink shoved it in his pocket with the rest of his cash. He must have made three hundred pounds in two hours.

'You steal books for that guy?'

'I am his biblioklept.'

I didn't know if he was being ironic or what with his words. Maybe he was a scholar. A junkie scholar. The thinking about it pressed my hangover. I was about to tell Stink that I'd go for vodka if he gave me a twenty but he was preoccupied with rooting out tinfoil and a cylindrical pipe from his pockets. He unwrapped cloud-yellowy heroin from cling film, pinched some off and sprinkled it onto the centre of the tinfoil.

'Stop looking at it,' Stink said. 'It will ruin you.'

'I already feel ruined,' I said but Stink was not listening. His lighter was in flame and held to the underside of the foil. The heroin sizzled and released smoke. He sucked it with his pipe then kicked back like London had stopped. I wanted that feeling. The beer was not working and I needed escape.

'It's my reason, see?' he said with a fleering grin.

I felt out in the cold with Stink tucked up so nice and tight in his heroin.

'Can I have a bit?' I said.

'No.'

'Go on.'

My forcefulness was wrecking his buzz. He shrugged. He had warned me, what more was there to be done? He sprinkled more onto the foil.

'Just get as much smoke as you can. Hold the pipe close and when it's all in, hold it.'

And just as this could all have been a different story, or no story at all, Stink spotted something behind me. 'Just wait a moment, Irish,' he said, shielding everything from sight.

A lad cycling a no-ordinary bicycle rolled passed us. It had three wheels, a backseat and an elderly couple sitting on it, enjoying the park and the sunny day.

'What's that?' I asked.

'Rickshaw,' Stink said.

'What? They give people lifts on them?'

'Mostly night labour when the tube's not running and homeward bound's a battlefield. They pick up scraps that are too drunk for the cabs or the tourists so incapacitated they forget what hotel they're staying at. Tough toil. Good customers for bike lights though.'

'Do you need a license for it or what?'

'You need to be a particular brand of crazy.'

'Is there a test?'

'Only the cabbies have their little test. *The Knowledge* they call it! The knowledge! If it's one thing not to equip a cabbie with, it's a test that they can pass called *The Knowledge*.'

'I'd like to do it,' I said. The lad seemed free and in-the-know, like he had things sorted. No boss, no fixed hours—have a few drinks, ride around the city, stop, drink, go again. It was perfect.

I handed the pipe back to Stink. I liked that the idea of the lad getting the elderly couple to where they needed to go. I liked that he was maybe bringing them home.

And I really needed to sort something out.

'Where can I get a rickshaw?'

'The poppy was a safer choice,' Stink said.

First Day

Rickshaws were to the back of the underground car park, hundreds of them, cable-locked through their front wheels like horses tied to a saloon rail. Crunched energy drink cans spilled from the bins and the sticky floor ripped at the soles of my shoes like Velcro.

There were two guys up ahead talking rickshaw.

'Arman?' I asked the smaller with the beady eyes.

'Yes,' he said.

'Stink said you might have a rickshaw for me.'

'This is my cousin, Zahir. He will start on the rickshaw tonight.'

Zahir was dressed in a suit two sizes too small for him, probably the biggest the shop had. He was eager, chomping at the bit for work. A big guy like him should have had a crushing handshake to show what a tough bastard he was but it was soft and barely there.

'I see you last night,' Arman said. 'You were shouting on Leicester Square. You are dumb.'

'What's with the suit?' I asked Zahir.

'He wants to make good business,' Arman said. 'Look good for customer.'

'I want to make good business,' Zahir said. 'Look good for customer.'

'Come, come,' Arman said, walking away. 'We will see Vasily.'

Zahir made sure he was ahead of me in the follow. He had a lunging walk, his thighs and shoulders too big for the rest of his body. They were both powerhouses and I was fat and drunk.

'Bullshit,' someone was shouting. 'Bullshit, bullshit, bullshit.'

'This will be Vasily,' Arman said. 'Very angry. Lights stolen from all rickshaw last night.'

Vasily was in his mid-twenties, barefooted and shirtless, leaping over the rows of rickshaws, kicking shredded tyre and throwing mangled wheels from his path. He picked up a vice grip and flung it into a shelf to explode washers and screws across the ground. A nest of mice ran for cover and Vasily kicked at them.

'Bullshit, how can I make business with this bullshit?'

On the walls of his enclosure were snapped chains hung from nails. There were shelves holding boxes of latches, hinges, cable ties, rubber mouldings, batteries, cable, and scraps of aluminium. There were bunches of Allen keys, wrenches, rolls of duct tape and Vasily the Russian thrashed through all of it.

'Who is this?' Vasily asked, pointing at me but not looking. Arman shrugged. I was on my own.

'I'm looking for a rickshaw,' I said. 'To rent.'

Vasily was suspicious. 'Where are you from?'

'Ireland.'

'No Ireland guys do this job, mate,' he said. He watched how I held myself, came close, looked at my blood-burst eyes then sniffed my chest. 'You drunk?'

'No.'

'Yes. You is drunk. I have bullshit enough with business. I give you bike when you is drunk and I will have bullshit one hundred times. No way, mate.'

It was a bluff, a false piece of morality for the record. This guy loved money. His Grandmother had been sold years ago.

'Who else rents rickshaws around here?' I asked.

'You have first week's rent and deposit?'

'I'll give it to you at the weekend when I make it from working.'

'Jesus Christ,' Vasily shouted. 'You see fucking red cross on front door?'

Arman shook his head and laughed.

'I'll pay you everything at the weekend. Sunday— the whole lot. If I don't have it by then, what have you lost?'

'I might lose bike.'

'You won't.'

'If I give you bike, and you do not come back with it, *I* will not chase you, I will call my friend who will chase you, and believe me, he will leave you where he find you. Do you understand?'

'I'll have the money by Sunday.'

'So Sunday, one hundred and eighty pounds?'

'No problem.'

'You will have to buy light—this junkie Stink bullshit bastard stole all this. You have this one,' Vasily said, slapping the rear end of a rusted shit-bucket, excommunicated from all the others, not even locked. Its handlebars were fucked and there was duct tape holding it all together. 'I call her *Big Bullshit.*'

Arman unlocked one of the shining rickshaws, speakers in the cabin corners for music, cushions and blankets all set up inside like a genie's lamp.

'You don't want to see my passport, get some details or anything?' I asked. I was trying to delay getting up on it, nervous, wanting some coaching, some anything, not just, *on you go then, good lad.*

'Passport? I can get you passport for fifty pounds,' Vasily said.

'Any tips then or what?'

'You have to watch the street and wait,' Vasily said, kicking bubble wrap out of his way. More mice hightailed it for safety. 'It like fishing. You can wait for big fish or catch lot of little fishes. Follow Arman and this new guy, see how they do business.'

I mounted Big Bullshit, clicking back gears hard like I thought I should then pedalled for half a turn before the chain fell loose.

'Stop, stop, stop. Don't change gear when bike is stop, Jesus Christ,' said Vasily, reaching under my leg to put the chain back on. 'Slowly.'

I took off again and crashed the back end into the lined-up rickshaws.

'Back is wider than the front with this bullshit.'

I pedalled up the ramp and out onto the street. I was banjaxed already. I wanted to stop for a drink and regroup. The front wheel hit potholes and pedestrians thought about crossing in front of me, stopped then made a break for it at the last second—traffic lights, signs, one-ways, cyclists, car alarms, big red buses. Arman was smiling back at me from on up the street, his pedalling solid, steady, and his back straight. He slowed to allow me catch up.

'Where's the other guy? Your cousin?'

'He has a lift. I will meet him in Soho.'

'He got a lift already? He's been doing it thirty seconds.'

'He is very good at business.'

Arman pedalled like he could have done it blind-folded and backwards. His angles and timing were all perfect as he weaved through the traffic, the backseat swishing on tight angles like a tailfin, ringing his bell to tease out a customer, asking everybody on the foot-paths, literally everybody—*Anyone lost, guys? Anyone need a lift home, guys?* He stood high on the pedals, a head above the crowd to allow an easier spot until he caught a fare from two women who wanted to go somewhere I never heard of before. They jumped on the backseat, excited. The hang of it was not just ped-alling. It was a whole other thing.

Arman cycled off and I found myself alone on Big Bullshit in the middle of London, knowing one street in the whole city—Oxford Street—because that was what the sign above my head told me it was called.

And streets only led to more streets. As soon as I had decided on one turn there were two more streets to chose from and the people kept coming and going, millions of them, the whole lot of them surging about in a direction of their choosing like it was no big deal.

'Anyone want a lift on this with me?'

Everybody kept going.

A double-decker bus roared an inch from my front wheel, so fast that its tailwind sucked the rickshaw forwards. The bus driver sounded the horn, scaring the bejesus out of me.

Fuck it, I jumped off and stood on the footpath looking at the thing, not knowing what to do next.

'Sorry, lad—these things fast?' a man asked to my side with a pure white head of hair, his accent Scottish and noble, a voice that let it be known it did not want a single bar of crap, its owner a grave and booming man.

'Very fast,' I said.

'We've to be at our car on Martin's Lane in ten minutes before it runs out of time and we get a ticket—can you do it?'

'Do you know where it is from here?' I asked off the cuff, hoping the question did not sound too stupid, as though it did not really matter, as though I was just making sure, hoping he would offer to direct me, turn-by-turn, inch-by-inch.

'*I* don't know, lad—look—can you get us there or no?'

I looked at him like he was on television, not saying yes, not saying no, wondering how the situation would unfold.

'This lad says he can do it, darling,' the Scot said to his wife who was trying to hail a black cab. She looked at me the way women do to detect bullshit, found it and told him so with a look.

'Come on now eh, quickly,' the Scotsman said.

She walked over with refinement, rushed for nobody, her heels hitting the ground like a hammer hitting glass, looking in my eyes to tell me she knew, and that time would tell.

We all got on the rickshaw.

'Ok, Martin's Lane here we come,' I said, trying to pedal but finding the rickshaw rooted. The back wheel was lodged against the curb, stuck by the new weight. I tried to walk-start it. The cabin rolled over the back of my ankle and trapped it underneath the weight.

'Bollocks,' I roared, the couple looking on, my foot in a serious amount of pain. I tried lifting the handlebars but the whole thing was heavy. Very heavy. 'Get off, get off, get off.'

'Us?' the Scot said to his wife. 'Does he want us to get off, is it?'

My ankle felt sprained and cut. Arman passed with new customers on his backseat. 'Never push start. You mess your ankles.'

'Are you all right?' the Scot asked.

'Yes,' I said, clearly not.

'Where are your lights?' asked the wife in a fine English accent that had sent men to the gallows in a previous life.

'Martin's Lane,' I said, summoning all my strength and pushing the rickshaw off my ankle.

'Is he all right?' asked the Scot.

'Physically or psychologically?' the wife asked back.

I chose a direction and away we went, my body flashing up sweats from the exertion. I had absolutely no idea where I was going. I looked to each street we passed, hoping *Martin's Lane* would appear somewhere in big neon lights. Two minutes passed.

'There should be theatres all around, eh,' the Scotsman said.

I took a left for no reason other than I had not turned in a while. Then a right. Then another right, turning back on to the street I had turned off.

'You sure you know where you're going, eh?'

'Yes, that's Bloomsbury Square there,' I said, pointing to a sign that said *Bloomsbury Square*. I cycled harder, thinking the more of London I covered, the sooner I would come across Martin's Lane. I clicked up the gears in one daring twist to show I was a serious rickshaw rider, professional, knowing all about gears but the jump was too much for Big Bullshit to cope with and the chain fell loose. The pedals went limp.

'Ah lad, lad, lad. What's going on, eh? What are you doing? Where are we?'

'It's fine, everything's fine. I just got to put the chain back on.'

'This ticket expires in two minutes.'

'No problem.'

The rickshaw came to a stop in the middle of a three-lane street. I got off and crouched under to pull the chain back on as Vasily had done earlier. My ankle needed ice and elevation.

'Get out that map,' the Scotsman said to his wife.

A double-decker bus came around the bend. Its horn roared.

The wife screamed.

'Christ Almighty,' yelled the Scot.

The bus slowed to a stop an inch from the front wheel and the bus driver pressed on his horn without release.

I got the chain back on, standing up to find the Scot getting off, telling his wife to do the same.

'It's just around here,' I shouted over the horn.

The Scot got back on the rickshaw, wanting to believe me. I cycled on, taking a madcap right turn down a road called *Gray's Inn*.

Horns sounded instantly.

'Fucking wanker,' shouted a cab driver out his window.

I wondered how it would look if I braked, got off and ran.

I could feel their stare on my neck and the beer was getting heavy in my stomach from all the pedalling.

Fifteen, great, big, lumping minutes passed. I became a bastarding ball of gag. The beer boiled in my stomach and gulped to the bottom of my throat. The crunched ankle was starting to stiffen and swell. I was practicing coming clean with an excuse like, *I thought you said St. Mark's Lane,* when a feeling like an electric shock shot up my hamstring and into my arse.

'My arse,' I shouted, grabbing it hard. It felt like a cheek had been ripped off. I forgot about steering and we swerved across the road into oncoming traffic. A car screeched to a sideways stop to avoid a collision.

'Just stop. Just FUCKING stop,' shouted the Scot, sounding as though he had not sworn in years. My face was burning. I leaned over the handlebars and dry- retched. I was winded with a sprained ankle and a paralysed arse. One of the pedals broke and my body fell with it, slamming my balls into the crossbar. I groaned like a dying cow.

'Are you drunk?' asked the wife.

'I've had one or two wine gums, Madam,' I said.

The driver of the car had made his way over and was screaming *wanker* in my ear. He wanted a punch-up but I didn't have the energy. The Scotsman got out as thunderously as he could, bashing off everything, the whole rickshaw shaking with anger. He helped his wife out and they stepped onto the footpath, turning around to see me spitting a long strand of sticky spit out the side of my mouth.

'An Englishwoman, an Irishman and a Scotsman all got on Big Bullshit,' I said then spewed up hot beer with the fizz still in it.

DIRECTIONS

Two riders sat on their rickshaws outside Covent Garden tube entrance. They must have been there for a reason. I braked to rest, to have a look and a slug of vodka. Beer was bad for pedalling. Vodka was better.

Both of the riders stared.

'It's for my arse,' I said. 'It's killing me.'

One said something to the other in Bengali. They both laughed.

People exploded out of the ticket hall—a crowd relentless and torrential, gushing, making the audiences across the West End, filling the pubs and clubs, a crowd that jostled, crammed and shoved past, that sucked the ATMs out of service. The two riders were there for some of that cash.

'You get nice office job, boss,' one said. 'This bad job for you.'

'Fat, drunk bastard,' said the other.

'I appreciate the honest feedback, fellas,' I said. 'Thanks.'

People stood looking around for direction for so long that space could not clear fast enough on the footpath and there were bottlenecks, packing the crowd back through the turnstiles, down the staircases and onto the platform below to delay trains.

Everybody was looking for somewhere, trying to find something; the theatre, the pub, a place to eat that wasn't too expensive but nice, a place where they could just sit down without loud music, a place *with* loud music, a jazz place, a pizza place, a metal bar, an open-mic night, a little Italian place with all the wine bottles on the wall—it went on and on. The lost all wanted help and I was bursting to oblige, bursting to know stuff, to have the expertise and capacity. I tried to make eye contact, to tell the lost I was there, a pleading type of look.

I straightened up and attempted to look knowledgeable and slim and happy and fit enough to pedal someone somewhere but I was obvious, as bamboozled as the rest of them.

Zahir rode past, a couple with deep tans on his backseat wearing *Notre Dame* sweatshirts, looking around at all of the lovely buildings, taking photos, enjoying themselves.

'Excuse me,' a nice old lady to my side asked. 'Is the Poetry Society Café around here?'

It was like Denise Dunne asking me behind the bike shed after school once—I was flattered she thought I was someone who knew something. I hopped off the saddle and took a look at a public map. 'We're facing this way so the Poetry Society Café, from here, would be down that street, a right, a left and then a right,' I reckoned, not too sure but vodka-brazen.

And with that, she walked away.

'Don't you want a lift?'

'Fuck off,' she called back.

London was tough.

There were people looking up to the tops of buildings to get a bearing, people on Google maps figuring out the way. An irritated girl was on her phone. 'Repeating the name of the street over and over is not helping me, Jonathan,' she said. 'No, stop repeating Langley Street. What's it near?'

The two Bangladeshis rolled away with people-filled backseats, confident and strong as though they had already arrived at their destination.

'Excuse me,' somebody said to my side. And on it went—some lost people admitting right off they did not want a lift, just directions. They smiled after I pointed to Leicester Square and said—'*Thanks very much, have a good night.*' Some said, '*Excuse me—Covent Garden Piazza?*' They did not break pace, wanting only reassurance that the direction in which they were walking was still good. They did not say thank you. Some people pretended to want a lift, asking off the cuff—'*Just which direction is Leicester Square so I know?*' Others gave you a choice—'*Lion King mate, that way or that way?'* Others thought of the direction-inquiring process as a much more confrontational affair.

'Nearest tube,' said a lad who got right up over the handlebars and in my face.

'That's a tube station just there.'

'Not that one. Tell me where the nearest tube station is.'

'Just there. I don't know any others.'

'Like fuck you don't,' he said. He was big with a long reach. I'd have to take him down by surprise and pummel him quickly.

Out of nowhere came Stink, 'Need any help with directions, sir?'

'The nearest tube that's not *that* one,' the lost and aggravated lad said.

'Straight down Long Acre here,' Stink said. 'Cross the intersection and Leicester Square tube station entry points will be right there. Could you spare a pound towards a bed and blanket, sir?'

'Are you're sure it's down that way?'

'Indeed, one hundred percent. A pound to help me out, sir?'

The aggravated lad walked down Long Acre like Leicester Square was in big trouble, whatever it had done.

'Some lost folk get embarrassed,' said Stink. 'Don't get involved. It's only when we are lost that we truly find ourselves.'

Stink got back to the crowd. 'Anyone lost there, folks? Anyone lost and need directions, folks?' People stopped and got where the Lion King was from him, handed him some coin and walked on.

'Anyone lost?' I asked the street.

'Oi,' Stink said. 'Find your own comically existential sales pitch.'

'Excuse me,' a girl in her early twenties said to my side. 'Would you do Kings Cross for a tenner?'

'Do you know where Kings Cross is from here?' I asked.

'I'll direct you. For a tenner, yeah? Vicki, this guy'll do it for a tenner,' she said, making eyes at Vicki to stop looking so surprised. I was excited and ready-to-go. There was a place ahead of us called King's Cross where the three of us wanted to be, somewhere behind us where we did not want to be, and me pedalling worked in favour of both agendas. The girls giggled and whispered and I was probably the one being taken for the ride but I did not care.

'So tell me more about Roland,' Vicki said.

'Well, he's in television. So that's kind of cool. But he's just green— romantically.'

'That's cute,' Vicki said.

'I'm too old for all that now. I need someone trained up already. You know? Take a right here, Rickshawboy.'

I pedalled on hard.

'This is Kings Cross,' they said eventually, gave me the tenner and hopped off.

I felt purpose and reason. Getting them to where they needed to go felt good. Then I looked around and all the streets looked the same and I couldn't remember which one I had come from. I picked a direction and charged for it, making madcap turns, lefts and rights until I was lost. I braked for a pick-me-up, spotting a Rastafarian inside a telephone box across the street. He was smoking a cone, the whole box cloudy dark. He drank from a can of high percentage lager in the same hand as the joint. Four empty cans of the same brand were aligned in a neat row on the shelf beside him.

'You know which way the West End is from here?' I shouted over to him.

He opened the telephone box's door and said, 'All roads go the same place.'

'Philosophically?'

'Yes,' he said then drank from his can.

I had my first pint when I was fourteen years old, sitting in the snug of Phelan's like a big man, sleeves rolled back, all the ale-drinking aul lads around, saying that the apple never falls too far. In Phelan's there were black and white photographs of all the dead and buried men of Ballybailte hung up on the walls, creamy pints of stout in front of them, looking at the camera the way men ought to look, coming from a time when men were men, put up by old Gerry Phelan to point you in one direction—a life drowned in drink. And by the dead and buried's faces, you'd think maybe they all had the right idea, slog it back, worry about it later.

I went upstairs after my fourth pint and jumped out the top window of the pub just for the laugh. I met Joanna Kennedy out on the street and we went up to the tennis court to kiss. I escorted her back down to the chippers afterwards and had a fight with Seany Lee because he used to go with Joanna. Seany was two years older and harder than long division. He had dropped out of school a year earlier to chain-smoke and drive tractors. He gave me a black eye with a huge punch that started life back at breakfast. I watched it coming and went down like a sack of spuds. Joanna started to slap him across the face and told him it was definitely over. It was the most excitement I had ever had in my whole life. I wore the black eye around like a badge of honour for the next week in school.

'Out in Phelan's having a pint,' I told the lads in woodwork. 'Went off with Joanna Kennedy then Seany Lee went mental.'

'Jaysus,' they said, wanting my story for themselves so they could tell people something, anything. That's how drinking started—excitement. I couldn't remember there ever being a choice about it. Lads who didn't drink, didn't have mad stories to tell in woodwork. The amount of pints one drank on any given night was a big talking-point as well as vomiting in unusual places, ending up in unusual places without memory of how you got there, and to drink other, more seemingly experienced drinkers under the table was the big one. If you didn't know all the

Gardaí and the town's juvenile liaison officer on a first name basis, you were a mug. And then drinking all started to feel like a fall.

I could not remember when I first slipped.

I could not remember when it all got bad and then got worse.

I could not remember when beer became spirits. I could not even remember how long I had been falling. Days had span on into months that span around and around into years.

I was drinking to avoid hangovers, my life was burnt to the ground and I was lost on a rickshaw somewhere near King's Cross, trying to get away from it.

The Rastafarian lost interest, closed the telephone box door and slid a finger inside the coin drawer to check for forgotten change.

I cycled on.

BIRTHDAY BOY

The rickshaw thing was over. I could not do it.

It was 4am, Sunday morning. I was pedalling back to the underground car park having spent three nights going from lost in one area of London to being completely lost in another. The £10 from my first and only fare was all I had. My ankle was killing me. I had pulled all sorts of muscles and spewed more times than I could count.

Fuck it.

More power to those riders full of energy but I was zapped, wasted, barely able to speak, openly slugging vodka as I pedalled, wanting to be caught by cops so that they would take it away from me, lock me up, give me a bed.

The Saturday-nighters on Oxford Street were lost, drunk and stranded too, unable to tell east from west, left from right.

'Back to my hotel, please,' shouted a desperate looking fellow. He was in bright red trousers and shiny-blue loafers, carrying a tweed suit jacket with brown leather elbow patches. The fellow waved to a black cab and it stopped beside him. The cabbie nodded and the fellow made to open the back door but found it locked. The black cab sped away, the fellow's hand still on the handle and was dragged a few steps by the force.

'You pig of a man,' he shouted at the taillights. 'Back to my hotel. It's the Holiday Inn. Someone, please.'

I knew the Holiday Inn. It was right beside the BT Tower.

I braked beside him. Some guys in tracksuits looked the poor bastard up and down and laughed. The fellow smiled along with them, not realising *he* was the joke.

'I know the Holiday Inn,' I said to him. 'I'll take you up there.'

'Top stuff,' he said. 'Let me get some cash out of the hole in the wall and we'll be on our way. It's my birthday today.'

I never celebrated my birthday. Birthdays could fuck off.

'Happy Birthday,' I said.

A short guy in a leather jacket stopped beside Birthday Boy, faking drunk, out on Saturday night but not a Saturday-nighter. 'Hello, my friend,' he said to Birthday Boy.

'Hello,' Birthday Boy said. 'Maze around here. Just employed this chap to bring me to my hotel.'

The guy leaned on the wall of the bank, pretending to write a message on his phone, stealing glances out the side of his face at Birthday Boy's wallet.

'I'm a ninny-hammer,' Birthday Boy shouted. He gave the PIN another try.

'Need help?' the guy asked.

'No thanks, old chap. Under control.'

I kept my stare right up in the guy's face. He gave me one back, telling me to stay out of it or I might not leave it.

'Bugger, bugger, bugger,' Birthday Boy shouted, turning back for the rickshaw. The guy swooped close, pinching into the pocket of his jacket for the wallet, failing but only just. He began a long-lost friend routine, putting his arm around Birthday Boy's neck, planning another try.

'Get out of here,' I said.

He released his arm from around Birthday Boy and came close to the rickshaw, threatening, squaring up and unafraid. He pressed his fist slowly into my face. I slapped him hard across the head with an open palm and hopped off the saddle.

'Next one's a closed fist,' I said and we just stood there, nobody backing down.

He charged for me and I gave him the next one. He tried a kick. I caught his foot, swept the other out from underneath him then put my foot on his face. I admired his confidence. He must have stood in front of his mirror for two hours every morning telling himself he was an unstoppable force with which to be reckoned.

'Chaps, chaps, chaps,' Birthday Boy said, hands on his hips, baffled.

'Get on,' I said. He did.

I took my foot off the guy, made sure he didn't try anything again, hopped back up on the saddle and cycled on.

I could hear Birthday Boy thinking in the back. He moved, stopped, moved again.

'Was that chap trying to rob me?'

'He went for your wallet.'

'You just saved my life—he would've killed me. What a shit birthday. That guy would've killed me. *And* I entered the wrong PIN three times so the machine's taken my card—I have thousands and thousands of pounds that I can't touch and my friend has pissed off on me. And it's my birthday. I'll call my so-called friend and get money from him to pay you.'

I cycled on.

'Richard—I've just been attacked,' Birthday Boy cried down his phone. 'A little foreign person has just tried to rob me. My rickshaw chap saved me. I need money to pay him upon arrival back at the hotel. Go to the ATM then. I can't. Because I entered the wrong PIN three times on my card and it's my birthday and you pissed off. I think he's Irish—what's your name driver?'

'Irish.'

'Irish, his name is Irish. No, he is Irish and he's also Irish. A rickshaw driver, Richard. Please, Richard OK? Please, OK? Happy? Thank you. Goodbye.'

I cycled up Great Portland until it became one-way then cut through sleepy streets until the green Holiday Inn glow came into view.

'Shit, bugger, shit,' Birthday Boy said. 'It's not the right hotel, Irish. I'm just going to kill myself.'

'Ring Richard—ask him what Holiday Inn,' I said, swinging round.

'Richard, what hotel is it? There's more than one. Because it's a chain, Richard. We're lost and I'm having the worst night of my life and I've decided I'm going to kill myself. Just call me back when you find out.'

Birthday Boy phoned more people.

'Where exactly are you?' his sister screamed down the phone so loud I heard it up front. My heart went out to her. I thought of my own sister. It was all the same old stuff, and nothing was original.

'London. London Road, London,' Birthday Boy said. 'Well that's as much as I can tell you, Phillipa. I would but the hotel I checked into this afternoon no longer exists. I'm going to kill myself.'

'Take it easy,' I said over my shoulder.

'Look, I have to go,' he said and hung up on her.

'When I kill myself Irish, you may have my thousand pound watch and my I-phone as payment.'

'Look up your Holiday Inn on your phone. You have an email booking receipt don't you? Google-map it.'

'OK—OK, good,' said Birthday Boy. 'Good.'

I heard him fumbling and finger-punching about on the phone.

'OK, left up here, straight, straight on—this is good. Good—keep going, left.'

The directions brought us past Bentley showrooms, an art gallery with bits of driftwood in the window and restaurants that didn't have their names on the front. Workers were about now with sleep still on their eyes, early risers for Sunday morning shifts. The day buses were beginning. The green neon of the Holiday Inn brand shone again at the top of the street.

'Richard, have you got money? Good. I owe my man. We're coming up to it now. Bugger. Bugger. Bugger. Because it's the wrong Holiday Inn again, Richard. That's it—I'm killing myself—Goodbye Richard.'

The back right wheel bumped and the pedalling felt immediately empty. I looked behind to find Birthday Boy lying on the street, holding his leg, crying. I circled back, got off the rickshaw and pulled him up by the scruff of his neck. He applied dead weight. I shook him about. 'Stop telling people you're going to kill yourself,' I shouted. 'You know what that does to people? Stop it, stop it right now.'

I wanted to get him home then it would be OK. Everything would sort itself out from there.

'Look. I'm going in here to get directions to the closest Holiday Inn that's not the Great Portland branch. That'll be yours. Don't follow me in, wrap yourself up in that blanket and just take it easy.'

'OK—OK, Irish,' said Birthday Boy. He curled up in the blanket, falling asleep almost instantly.

I walked through the lobby of the *Mayfair* Holiday Inn en route to the front desk when one of the elevator doors opened. A young woman dressed in a white bathrobe stormed out, crying, mascara running.

'I'm going to fucking kill you,' she shouted to the hotel's night manager who was accompanying her, trying to hold her arm. 'And get your fucking hands off me.'

I made the mistake of looking at the commotion a split second too long.

'And what the fuck are you looking at?'

'Lovely language for a Sunday morning,' I said. 'Off to mass?'

'Fuck you,' she screamed and charged for me, held back by the night manager.

'Can I help you, sir?' the receptionist said.

'I'll kill everyone,' shouted the angry young woman.

'Where's the closest Holiday Inn, not the Great Portland Street one?'

'Don't fucking look at me again,' the angry young woman said to the back of my head.

The receptionist was on Google Maps about to sort out the whole situation when in walked Birthday Boy, the blanket across his shoulders like a cape, his eyes red and his face raw having flash-slept for ten seconds. The bright lights of the lobby were confusing him.

'Thanks Holiday Inn you shower of absolute bastards,' he shouted. The Holiday Inn stayed calm.

'Thank you, mate,' shouted the angry young woman as though validated, as though someone was finally talking some sense. Birthday Boy moved over to where she had been instructed to sit in wait for the police. The pair locked eyes.

'Worst night of my life,' Birthday Boy said. 'Wrong PIN, mugged, no money, friend pissed off, hurt my leg and now I'm completely lost.'

'They're dreaming if they think I'm paying for a new television or an ice machine,' the angry young woman said.

'Absolute bastards,' Birthday Boy whispered.

'Total bastards,' confirmed the angry young woman and leaned in. Birthday Boy made his move and the two locked mouths, inserted tongues and began petting in the space of a second. Birthday Boy dropped the blanket to the ground and tried to find gaps in her bathrobe.

'OK Miss, in here please,' said the night manager from the office behind reception.

'This cunt,' she said to Birthday Boy.

'Hey, where's my fucking hotel?' shouted Birthday Boy to the night manager, coming to the defence of his fair maiden.

'Sir, if you're not a guest in this hotel could you please leave,' the night manager demanded.

'You can come to my hotel with me when this rickshaw chap finds out where I'm located,' Birthday Boy said to the angry young woman.

I got Welbeck Street from the receptionist's screen.

'I'll give you a closed fist, you cunt,' shouted Birthday Boy.

I pulled Birthday Boy outside to the porch but he shirked me off and gave the glass door a running kick only to rebound off of it and fall flat on his arse.

'You're an embarrassment,' I said.

'I think I could have had her,' said Birthday Boy. 'Could've made a decent end to a shit night—my birthday today, Irish.'

'Just shut up and get on,' I said.

I cycled up one-way streets back to Oxford Street, hoping each new set of oncoming headlights did not belong to the cops. Birthday Boy was in the foetal position in the backseat, shivering. I pedalled with every ounce of strength left, my heart beating hard enough for the two of us.

On Oxford Circus I went north.

'Worst night of my fucking life,' shouted Birthday Boy, kicking the side of the rickshaw in tantrum.

'I'm looking for Welbeck Street. Just shut up so I can concentrate. If you kick the rickshaw again, I'm bringing you down to the Thames and throwing you in.'

'Good.'

I cycled down Wigmore Street and met Welbeck that cut across it, took a left and pulled up to the front steps of Birthday Boy's Holiday Inn.

'You need to take it easy,' I told him.

'Come up to the room. Once I reach safety I will not want to return to the street.'

I followed him through the front doors, into lobby and into the elevator. A receptionist pretended to mind his own business. Each to their own, his eyebrows said. The mirrors sparkled, not a blemish on the trimming or carpet— everything pristine except the reflections of the bedraggled Birthday Boy and sweat-soaked me.

'Why do you do that rubbish? The rickshaw. You must be the only one of them who speaks the lingo, surely. I mean, you're not an imbecile—you could get a job. I'll get you a job—ever been to Swindon?'

The elevator door opened on the fifth floor to a still and silent hallway. Birthday Boy strode over to number 503 and gave it an almighty kick. I made to calm him down.

'I can do what I want. We are not on the rickshaw anymore.'

Richard opened the door with one hand, the other hovering over the front of his underpants. Smoke wafted out from behind him. There were empty bottles with cigarette ends in their dregs all around the two single beds. A naked girl was in one of them wondering whatthefuck, and a gangbang

that looked like it was shot in the seventies was playing on pay per view, the volume uncomfortably loud.

'Jesus Christ, Richard. Let me in quickly.'

'What happened?' Richard asked.

'Oh not much, you abandoned me on my birthday then I was attacked by a gang of muggers who
wanted to kill me, did a tour of about fifty Holiday
Inns and but for this chap here I'd have been mur-
dered. Give him money.'

'How much does he want?'

'Hello,' Birthday Boy said to the naked girl.

'Hi,' she said back.

Birthday Boy sat on the bed beside her. 'What's
your name then?'

'A hundred,' I said.

'A hundred!' Richard said.

'Like he said, there were quite a few Holiday Inns
and I had to save him quite a few times from being
killed. There was a huge gang of muggers after him.'

'Jesus Christ!' Richard said. 'The rickshaw chap
wants a hundred!'

'Well give it to him then you cheap tonsil,'
Birthday Boy said.

Richard handed me five purple twenties.

'Thanks,' I said and turned towards the door.

'Baby, you all kinds of wrong,' said a gentleman
in the gangbang.

Zahir the Horse

Sunday's focus was already on night so as to get itself over with. It started to rain around the same time as I finished the vodka. The buildings slept into the afternoon. The traffic trickled and flags drooped around their poles. There were no pigeons, no life at all, as though the apocalypse had arrived and missed me. I parked up beside three Turkish rickshaw riders down on Piccadilly Circus.

We had no fares, nowhere to go. They passed around a joint but I didn't take it. They shrugged like it was my loss but I was slumped, muddy and full of horror as things were—wet socks to top it off. I needed a drink.

The four horses of Helios were down the street from us. They were statues, reared up on their hind-legs, restless, having rolled the sun from east to west everyday for centuries and then overnight they were bronzed and became just a story, something people looked at. Copernicus had ruined everything for them.

A citybreak couple wearing matching all-weather jackets and hats took photos of them then spotted our rickshaws and strolled over. I was not preoccupied with the whereabouts of the joint so they picked me to start a conversation. 'We were perhaps thinking that maybe a member of the royal family had died,' said the wife-half.

Norwegians I guessed.

'It's so quiet,' said the husband-half. 'I mean, compared with yesterday. No comparison.'

'No comparison,' agreed the wife-half. 'There is a nautical expression—dead calm—that is what the city is like now, no?'

'Yes. Dead calm is accurate,' said the husband-half. 'And after such a raging storm of yesterday. Today is flat.'

'Could you please perhaps take a picture of us with all of these lights in the background?'

They stood embracing, in love and having an amazing time in front of the lights of Piccadilly Circus, not knowing how lucky they were that Canon had never added a machine gun setting.

'You want a lift anywhere in my rickshaw?'

'How much would you charge us to Russell Square?'

'Ten,' I said, soft and quiet so the Turks would not hear how low I was going, feeling my eyes going funny, signals getting mixed, the Norwegians reading it like I was ripping them off.

I needed a drink. 'Ok, eight,' I said to try and save it. 'Eight's a bargain.'

'No thank you,' they said. 'We will walk.'

They hung around photographing more. The we-will-walk comment was to shake me off. I didn't blame them.

'My name is Kudret,' one of the Turks said. He was relaxed, high and loving life. 'I can take you to a very nice place good for Sundays.' The Norwegians hopped up on his backseat and they sailed away up Shaftesbury Avenue, meeting Zahir who was galloping his rickshaw towards us, chomping at the bit like traffic better watch out, his forehead maroon and sweating, his muzzle sucking in enough air for a submarine of men.

'I need another rickshaw,' Zahir said, not stopping his roll, stomping about in circles to the front of us, Krebs cycles bursting out his ears.

'No way,' the other riders said.

'Come on, come on, one more rickshaw,' Zahir shouted like it was life or death. The others looked away like he was a joke.

'You. Irishman. Come, come,' Zahir said then galloped back towards Coventry Street. I stood up on my pedals and cycled on to try and catch him.

It was movement so I was happy.

He waited for me at Leicester Square. At his flank were a group of nine women, none of whom had ever been shy of a biscuit.

'This the other one?' asked the leader of the women. 'And the two of you are doing it for fifteen each?'

'Where we bringing them?'

'Tower Hill,' Zahir said.

'Is Tower Hill not very far from here? For fifteen? Per person?'

'Per rickshaw,' Zahir said.

'Take it or leave it,' the women's leader said.

'There's nine,' I said.

'I will take five,' Zahir said. That was that. Five got up on the Zahir's backseat, pushing out the sides, piling up on top of one another, the women on the bottom getting lost inside, trying to peek their heads out through all the rump and shoulder. The remaining four got up on mine, including the leader who instructed two low-ranking women to sit across the backseat, then she and her deputy sat on their laps.

Zahir the Horse led the way down to Trafalgar, the ride downhill and gentle until we started the incline up the Strand. Zahir's broad back got low, aligning itself in perfect conformation with his knees and hindquarters for the most efficient pulling drive. I cycled on, trying to dig as deep as him to keep up, never before feeling as much resistance in the pedals.

Zahir got about twenty lengths in front.

'Looks like we got the dud, girls,' the leader said.

Zahir made light work of Aldwych.

The bristles on the leader's chins scraped the back of my neck as she leaned forward and breathed down my collar. 'Poor little fella can't handle all this woman. Maybe he prefers the men on his backseat? You think so?'

'Probably,' her deputy said.

'That's it I'd say,' said the leader. 'I'd say he'd be more than happy to have four big men back here. Look at him. He's sad. Don't worry darling, we'll get you a nice big man when we get down to Tower Hill. That can be your motivation. Pedal, pedal, pedal.'

The Australian High Commission and the Royal Courts of Justice passed us by, averting their attention, not saying a word, not wanting any part in the work. We took Fleet Street and began the run down to the intersection at the bottom.

Zahir made the green light and used the downhill momentum to get halfway up Ludgate hill to St. Paul's cathedral. The lights changed red before I got there, forcing me to brake dead at the bottom of the hill.

My body trembled. I felt terminal.

'You're fucked now,' the leader said and laughed about it as close to my eardrum as she could get.

The women in Zahir's rickshaw slapped his arse because he had to rear up off his saddle against the steep part of Ludgate. They yee-haw'ed and slapped away and Zahir only dug deeper.

'The girls have the right idea,' the leader said. 'Bit of motivation.'

The lights changed and I stood up off the saddle to pull the women up the hill. The leader went for my boxer shorts straight away, yanking them up to use as reigns.

I pulled them away from her hand.

'He didn't like that. Touchy, touchy,' she said and trailed one of her feet against the asphalt to cause friction and slow the ascent even further.

'*Flintstones, meet the Flinstones,*' she sang and the other women joined in. Zahir was gone, down at Tower Hill already probably. Wherever it was. I had no idea how to get there so I knew I had abuse coming about being lost. Sweat splashed off my face and my clothes soaked. My heart pumped painful shocks of electricity.

Then Ludgate Hill's steep gradient really kicked in. I pushed against the pedals, higher up Ludgate, bit by bit, rotation by rotation, ascending slower than a walk while getting slapped and teased and my bulldozer of a hangover pounded.

'They're the ones that don't go away in a day,' my father had said once. 'You go past five days and there's a bulldozer waiting.'

To get away from his voice I dug harder and deeper, taking pleasure in the pain, ticking over the Krebs cycles, flushing mitochondria with delicious energy and bang—back on track, the pain as good as a drink, better even.

JOSEPH

Drink-drivers in my hometown of Ballybailte were flagged down by the Gardaí, stepped out of their car and driven home by one Garda while the other would follow behind in their car and park it outside their house to have it there ready and waiting in the morning.

The local Gardaí were forced to swap towns it got so bad.

The Ballyragget cops had to come to Ballybailte to catch the drink-drivers and the Ballybailte boys had to go to Ballyragget. That's how I was caught—Ballyragget cops. There was already bad blood between the arresting Garda and I. He had bit me on the ground in a tussle in an U-16 County final ten years before. When he got up, I punched him back down then shown a red card.

After the drink-driving debacle, my sister, Niamh wanted to talk. I said OK. She suggested a drive, just the two of us. Niamh had settled down when she had kids. Once-was-wild-child now a sensible mum.

'Do you want to talk about him?' she asked.

She turned off the car engine and stared towards the doors of the Community Centre. I wanted to tell her everything, to spill it all so that she could carry it around on her shoulders, too.

'No,' I said.

'Maybe you can talk about it in there?' she said, and left the sentence hanging in the air. It all clicked—Friday night. The Community Centre.

'Fuck off, Niamh.'

A moment earlier I would have done anything for her but now I hated her. I didn't care if I never saw her again.

'I left you in that house with him after Mam died. And I swear to God, I'd do it different if I could. And I've been trying, Joe.' She started to cry. 'Whatever's going on, you need to talk about it with *someone*.'

'I'm fine.'

'Yeah, Joe, what was I thinking? Course you're fine.'

'I'm not going in there.'

'Joe, look, you're not staying with me if you're drinking. I can't expose the kids to what we were exposed to. I can't. So, you're going in there or you have find somewhere else. I'm sorry.'

'You're kicking me out?'

'It's all your leaving me with. I can't cope. I can't.'

Underneath it all, I didn't blame her for anything. I really didn't. But I used her guilt against her all the same. That's what happens when someone gets in the way—the addict throws anything they can back at them, usually the most hurtful and painful thing at hand. 'Well, Niamh, maybe if it's all getting too hard for you, you can fuck off back to Bondi Beach for another two years, hide out again.'

I got out of the car and slammed the door.

The Friday night alcoholics at Ballybailte's Community Centre were fixing their coffees when I walked inside. I took my shoulder of vodka from under my coat and slugged from it right up in their friendly faces as they took their seats around me. Their crisp clean shirts and non-judgemental expressions annoyed me.

I slugged more vodka.

'Hello there, new man. I'm the Chairman,' Terry Deegan said. Terry drank a bottle of whiskey one lunchtime then knocked down his house with a JCB in the afternoon so that the bank couldn't have it.

There were characters and lunatics in my town, lads who were always one spit from self-annihilation, simpletons who could tell you every score of a Manchester United game since there was Manchester United but couldn't tell you the day of the week. They were whom people aspired to be, people with quirks and weirdness, people who knew what it all would take but just couldn't be bothered. There was no cinema, no shopping centre, no bowling alley or museums. There was no snooker hall even though all Noel Dempsey ever did was walk up and down the two streets of the town with his snooker cue, looking for one.

People were the entertainment.

'What's the story, Terry Deegan?' I said and laughed.

'How long've ya wanted off the drink, Joe?' said one of the alcoholics. Cathal Gahan was his name. Everyone knew Cathal. A year before, he was pissing himself outside the chippers every night, crying about his wife leaving him to anyone who would listen.

Gahan's words though—off the drink—scared me. Off the drink? What did people do off the drink? Where did they go? What was someone's whole life pointed at if they were off the drink?

'The idea of these meetings are to cater for people who want to stop drinking, Joe,' Terry said. 'The fact that you're wet right now is not a problem. And nobody here is going to wrestle that bottle from you. Nobody can make you stop. You have to *want* to do it. It might be scariest thing you've ever imagined doing. It certainly was for me.'

'Wet?' I said, not liking the way the sound rolled off Terry's tongue. 'What are you saying wet? Who's wet?'

'It's a term for someone who's been drinking.'

'Here,' I said and offered the Terry the bottle. 'Want to be wet?'

'OK, that's enough,' Gahan said. 'It's not fair on the group to have him drinking that in here.'

'I heard the wife is having a grand old time in Gran Canaria, Gahan. I heard she's one of them cougars now,' I said, thinking I was hilarious, pot-valiant with all the vodka taken, equipped to take on the world.

'What did you say?'

'Cathal, please,' Terry said.

'Here, *Cathal*,' I said, offering him the bottle. 'Take a drink.'

Gahan launched himself out of his chair and went for me. I stood to meet him, finding his anger all too funny. I grabbed his scruff with pleasure and he grabbed mine. He gave me a punch across the chin. I gave him one back and then I was taken down, held at my arms and legs. Someone had taken a hold of my earlobe and was trying to rip it off. The blood vessels inside it cracked. I laughed and loved every second of it. It felt soft there in the middle of the ruck with the world burning down around us—they could have put it in a painting.

Gahan took a cheap shot across my chin to get the last word. He was pulled away and began to cry. 'It's just so fucking hard,' he said, over and over.

The alcoholics used my head to open the emergency exit door and threw me out into the car park. I found it hilarious.

'Come back next meeting, Joe. Please,' Terry said.

'Go 'way to be fucked,' I said, opened my vodka and took a swig in his face then walked on, laughing to myself, happy I had ruined their meeting and delighted to have upset Gahan. They shut the door.

I thought I was brave and righteous, a saviour of something, having upper-handed a bully.

I kicked the wing mirrors off of all the alcoholics' cars. They popped and crunched and some dangled by the side doors. I felt like a sophisticated criminal, a ninja, somebody with something to do, somebody with a purpose. I called Niamh to come get me.

'How did it go?' she said.

I did not reply and she knew.

'You're drunk. You've been drinking? Yes?'

'Yes.'

'That's just brilliant. Well, don't come back here. Do you hear me? Don't come back here, Joe. I'm not opening the door.'

'I'm sorry.'

'I know you're sorry. I know. But I'm not having you here around the kids. So find somewhere else. That's it.'

GOAT FISHING

Vasily was standing over me when I woke. I took all of the money from my pocket and handed it over in a sweaty ball.

'I want to die,' I said.

'Wait until heart palpitation.'

My ears were broken from the constant police and ambulance sirens out on the streets. 'Heart what?'

'Heart is pumping blood in your body very fast. I got a murmur. I cannot pedal anymore.' He pointed to a scar on his chest. 'Keyhole surgeries. I nearly die. Happen very many guy in this business.'

He counted the money. 'You is fifty-five short. Did you look at how Arman does business?'

Arman rode an Ecopromo rickshaw with no plexiglass cover in between him and the customer, prestigious amongst the Bangladeshis because with no plexiglass, fares could be raised en route by showing tourists the sights. Every night, Arman sat on the back of his rickshaw in Soho Square, surrounded by Zahir and other newbie Bangladeshi guys who huddled around his cube-shaped head like it was a television, banking every word he said. Arman was their leader and always counted through a wad of cash in front of them to make sure they knew it. The newbies could not tell interesting stories and lie about the fare because their English was poor so until it improved, they opted for the Ecopromo *with* a plexiglass hard-top. It only had one benefit of attracting girls who had just straightened their hair and did not want it frizzling in the rain. These girls were plentiful on both Oxford and Regent Street, working out well for the newbies because here the fares had plainer directions—up, down, stop, go.

'Cube-headed bastard showed me nothing,' I said.

'Can you write English?' Vasily asked.

'Yeah.'

'So write me letter and you can owe me rest of monies next week.'

'Letter?'

'Fucking cabbie bullshit on my business,' he said, flinging me an *Evening Standard.* 'Page four.'

There was a photograph of a rickshaw, mangled and flattened underneath a London bus on page four.

London Cab Authority Conduct Rickshaw Safety Experiment read the headline. *Crash a rickshaw at 30 miles per hour, with dummies inside. See what happens to the dummies,* said Jamie, an interviewed London cabbie. The London Cab Authority then followed Jamie's advice and spent £15,000 for a scientific experiment to show the public just what would happen to them if a rickshaw crashed at 30 miles per hour. The rickshaw got obliterated. The article directed the reader to the video of it on YouTube where they could watch a dummy's head come off its shoulders.

'Safety,' Vasily said. 'They says safety! At us! Three hundred dies every year on black cabs.'

'So what's the letter?' I said.

'Letter is to the Evening Standard bastards,' he said and handed me his work-in-progress.

> '*Dear you Evening Standard bastards,*' it read. '*You no nothing. Your story is for the cabbys and is bullshit and discusting. They are rapists. I am rickshaw owner and I will strike down upon you with grate vengense and fureos anger thoos who attempt to poisun and distroy my rickshaw.*'

'Have you been watching *Pulp Fiction*, Vasily?'

'Yes.'

'Maybe try a different approach.'

'This is what I want. A different approach.'

I took his pen and restarted.

> '*Dear Editor,*' I wrote, '*As an owner of rickshaws and secretary of the London Rickshaw Council, I was absolutely delighted with your article in yesterday's paper. Safety has been our top priority since the beginning but unfortunately, we never had the funds for scientific investigation. Could you please*

extend our gratitude to the London Cab Authority for their whopping donation of £15,000 into the matter? It was both Christmas and Birthday all rolled into one for our engineers yesterday on seeing the laboratory experiment. As I write, they are reinforcing differentials, strengthening crossbars and fitting seatbelts to the whole fleet. The experiment added insight in ways we genuinely could never have imagined. If I could, I would return the favour to the London Cab Authority for a scientific investigation of their own, what with over 300 fatalities a year in London alone involving black cabs. At the moment unfortunately, all I can offer is my warmest thanks and have them know that I am in their debt. Yours Sincerely, Vasily.'

'What it means?' asked Vasily.

'War probably,' I said.

'Good,' he said, and away he went in a flurry of bedlam. 'There is this fucking sandwich,' he said, finding a BLT on top of his toolbox. He took a bite then left it back down. 'Irish,' he said, 'I have new rickshaw for you—fifteen kilos more light—maybe twenty. I gave you Big Bullshit because I thought you would crash it into Thames. You was drunk. You is not drinking anymore?'

'No,' I said. 'I gave up.'

'Good with this bullshit,' Vasily said and slapped the saddle of the new rickshaw. That was that.

I got up out of Big Bullshit and hopped up on my new rickshaw. It felt lighter the second I pushed on the pedal, accelerating as though it was a regular bike. I turned fast, putting it up on two wheels then swerved back to Vasily.

Arman arrived, looking happy to witness the moment when I found out I had been pedalling a Volkswagen around London.

'Monday is OK for business sometime,' Vasily said, chasing mice. 'Guys are tired. Not many rickshaws go out on Mondays. Arman, take him. Show him. This fucking mouses, I hate them.'

'Mice,' I said.

'What?'

'One mouse. Two mice.'

'It is thousand mouse.'

'A thousand mice.'

'Go and make monies. Arman!'

'Busy, boss.'

'This bullshit. Show him. Now.'

'OK, boss,' Arman said, looking at me like I had just pointed to him from a witness box, mounting his Ecopromo, riding out. 'Come, come,' he called.

I hopped up on my new rickshaw and followed.

Arman gave me the silent treatment for four or five streets, cycling hard, breaking red lights, whizzing in and out between bumpers on Oxford Street, then zipped the wrong way down Wardour Street. When we reached Old Compton and he found he hadn't lost me, he braked then sat with his feet up on his handlebars outside Fahim's kebab shop.

'People don't want to ride in rickshaw. We are not a taxi—we are more expensive. More cold. More precarious. And some people feel exploitative. Yes?'

'Precarious and exploitative?' I said. 'A minute ago all you could say was, *yes boss, very good boss.*'

The different crowds were all around us looking for the restaurant, the theatre, the pub, the gig, everyone desperate for direction. Arman point-blank refused to help unless they took a lift with him. I did what I could—pointing in the direction of Piccadilly, or the nearest tube, or Soho Theatre.

'The UK imports millions of pounds worth of goat meat from India and Australia and Pakistan each year. But where are all the goats?' he asked, raising his palms theatrically, looking around the street. 'Here goat, goat, goat. Where are you, goat? I don't see any goats. Do you?'

'You look like a goat with a square head,' I said.

'You look like fat, Irish goat,' Arman said. 'All of the goat meat is over there in Fahim's being called lamb.'

Arman pushed on his pedals and cycled on in darts. I followed. As he moved he examined expressions then tracked back on the same groups in two minutes time to check on their progress.

'Monday is bad night,' he called over his shoulder before heading for Covent Garden.

He eventually braked outside the tube station beside five lads, mid-twenties, looking around, debating which way was what. They were all a bit out of style, dressed for summer even though it was winter. The high street shops were all shuttered-up but punters still spilled out of the tube station in bursts and walked down Long Acre.

'How are you all tonight?' Arman said.

'We're good, mate.'

'What's wrong, boss? You want a hug?' Arman said to the tall one, the most dejected-looking, booze having brought him to that sour and sulky place. The others bucked up, impressed by the daringness and not wanting to be the next to be set upon by Arman.

'Mate, we're just looking for a good pub or club or whatever—anything like that around?'

'Many bar like this. boss. But around here it is all guest-list.'

'That's all we got over the weekend—guest-list and all that shit. So there's no place we can go?'

'Brixton, Islington,' Arman said. He could have said Mars and Neptune for all the names meant to the lads. The street got that bit colder to them. They curled up inside their pockets that bit more.

'Fuck this,' said the tall one.

There was a silence and Arman let it hang for a few seconds.

'I do know one place, boss. Open until six in the morning. Free alcohol for first hour.'

'Where's that?'

'Not far.'

'And it's free alcohol?'

'For first hour, yes boss. Once you pay admission it is free alcohol for first hour. Have five drinks and you make back admission. If you are not distracted by beautiful girl.'

'There's nice girls there?'

'Very beautiful girl. Very beautiful. Yes, boss. Taking their clothes off all around.'

'Strip club is it?'

'Gentlemen's club,' Arman said, smirking.

They smirked back. 'And how far is it?'

'Not far—this way—we can take.'

'And how much is it in?'

'Thirty-five. But free alcohol for first hour. Drink many drink, yes? And you can touch girl in private dance. Touching is OK.'

'And how much do you want for bringing us there?'

'Twenty per bike.'

'No way, mate.'

'Fifteen is good, boss.'

The five of them looked at each other and began to rile themselves up.

'Let's do it,' one said and that was that.

Two got on my rickshaw, three went with Arman who led the way, through the small streets of Covent Garden at a snail's pace, rounding Bow Street, backtracking and hitting Bow Street again, puffing and huffing, his gears set high and slippery to give the effect of work.

'And you can touch the girls, mate?' asked a lad in my backseat.

'Yes,' I said. 'You can.'

'And it's free booze for the first hour, mate?'

'Yes,' I said. 'It is.'

Arman turned onto Parker Street. We rolled to a stop, Arman looking like he had just completed the tour de France. The strip-club bouncer welcomed the lads with a big friendly smile, opening the door for them and lead them inside to reception. They had gone from out-of-place, out-of-towners to royalty.

'It's all fabrication,' Arman said when they were out of earshot. 'The free drinks are through table service—waitress will only make one trip and if they do not tip with a note she will not come back. After that, tipping her is just like buying the drink.'

'Still,' I said. 'They looked happy.'

'The ladies that sit on their laps will want drinks, too but are not be included in the free drink deal. And the ladies will want champagne—watered down by the bartender so that they don't get drunk when they order five each. They pour most of it into the plastic plants anyway—drunkest plants in London.'

'Anything else?'

'The place is actually opened until six but it will cost a down payment on a house to stay here until then. Sometimes it does.'

'And touching the girls?'

'Touch a girl and they get their arm broken. It is a failsafe lie. Nobody verifies the ability to touch the girls with doormen.'

'Where is this vocabulary coming from?'

'Smart people know what dumb people want,' said Arman.

The bouncer came back out from reception and walked over. 'Who wants it?'

'I will take it,' Arman said.

'Five blokes at thirty-five pounds each,' said the bouncer, 'Comes to a hundred and seventy-five pounds. Just sign that there for me then, fella.' He held a receipt book out in front of Arman who had a pen at the ready.

'Thank you,' Arman said, handing back the receipt book, taking the cash and counted it to make sure it was all there.

I had no idea what was going on.

'You get their admission as a commission,' Arman said. 'Only in the strip clubs on the outskirts that do not get the tourist trade. You bring them customer, they give you the customer's admission.'

'Only if they've never been here before,' the bouncer said.

'Only if they've never been there before,' Arman said.

'Don't I get some of that?' I said, pointing at the cash.

'No.'

'He brought two didn't he?' the bouncer said.

'First time,' Arman said.

The bouncer nodded and walked back to the door. Arman waved the cash in my face, fanning me with it.

'Greedy little bastard,' I shouted to him as he cycled off.

'I've just taught you how to fish you dumb motherfucker. And you want a bite of my fish, too?'

I cycled back the Seven Dials, a roundabout where seven different roads all converged. Leicester Square, Trafalgar Square, Soho and Covent Garden tube station were all in short walking distance but it did not seem that way when tourists stood there on the cobbles peering down dark streets for direction. People went up one street and came back up another, trying another, coming back, trying another, getting angrier and angrier with one another for not being able to follow the map, handing it to the other—'*You bloody find it then if you're the expert cartographer.*'

I was alone and shaking and missing vodka. I thought about the feeling of hot, raw spirit rushing down my throat and into my belly. Vodka was in the shops all around, and the people manning them would've had no idea that that was the day I had decided to stop drinking. They would smile and hand me the bottle, thank me very much and wish me a good day.

And then, just like that, two lads appeared that I would not have known to approach before Arman's tutorial, both a bit out of style, still dressed for summer even though the weather was winter, looking around debating which way was what.

I pedalled over to the two lads and braked, smiling as though I meant it, looking the way men ought to look, coming from a time when men were men.

'What's wrong, fella?' I asked the more miserable of the two. 'Want a hug?

HALLOWEEN

I'd been watching riders all October. Watching was key, noticing what happened out on the street, studying how they stayed busy, trying to pick things up in an occupation where everyone wanted newcomers to fail. Groups were mainly formed on nationality—the Turks, the Colombians, the Bangladeshis. Since I was the only Irish rider, my group was comprised of me, and only me. New riders came and went. Anyone could do it for a day or a week but little nods of acceptance started after a couple of months, only when riders had passengers, for two reasons. Firstly, it was a bragging right. A nod meant, *look at me and my passengers you fare-less fool.* Secondly, when there were passengers on board, it was the only time a rider could really focus on anything else.

I had learned about musical bursts. Simple enough—tourists went to musicals. When they exited the theatre at certain times of the night there were high concentrations of them in one spot who did not know London and had disposable cash to spend on rickshaws.

London was a disguise, a place to hide, to be somebody else if you wanted. Halloween seemed to embody it.

'I can give you a lift?' I said to the three Wallys outside Leicester Square tube station. They were the whole shebang—red and white stripy jumpers, bobbled beanies, blue pants, round specs, brown shoes and each holding a walking cane.

'No thanks, we'll walk,' the first Wally said. 'In which direction is it though?'

'Well—you go up, cross all the way over to the other side and that will take you over to the Palace which is not to be confused with the Cambridge Theatre that's not actually on Cambridge Circus if you'd believe. Then take the cobbles onto Old Compton, Moor Street it's called, and then the next right and it's right there on your left—Greek Street.'

I had been learning the London Street Guide off by heart.

'I think he's talking about Cambridge.'

'I heard Cambridge, too.'

'No, Gate 68.'

'And don't take Shaftesbury Avenue,' I continued. 'That's on the left off Charing Cross that brings you all the way down to Piccadilly Circus, nowhere near where you want to go. Not even a circus. Just means circle.'

'Levy said it was just up from Leicester Square,' said the second Wally. I rolled my eyes at that Levy fellow. The misinformationist. The exaggerator. The liar.

'So, you could bring us?' said the second Wally like he had thought of it all on his own.

'Hop on,' I said, carrying them up to Old Compton Street, a gay friendly zone—guys in the green Britney dress carrying the white snake around their necks, guys as cheerleaders and naughty nurses. There were builders in tight hot pants but they were shy and kept mostly inside the pubs, sinking pints. The lesbians up outside Candy Bar were mainly Chicago gangsters from the roaring twenties with penciled moustaches and oversized Tommy guns.

More Wallys surfaced from the underground in the next hour, wandering about in twos and threes, waving to each other from across streets, combining forces in search of Gate 68, trotting about Chinatown and Charing Cross Road, getting picked off by other riders as they got wise to the Wally fare, too. It was easy—little fishes—short runs, their destination ready for them on first contact.

A pirate approached me looking like he had been shanghaied in the West End. His cutlass was broken and he looked worse for wear. His beard was smudged and he was on the verge of tears.

'Oi,' he started with, 'Where is this?'

'Shaftesbury Avenue.'

'Aw, fuck off,' he said and marched off. He was an angry pirate.

A giant party of Oompa Loompas hurled from pub to pub kicking each other up the arse—forty grown men in green wigs, white dungarees, all of them caked in orange paint. Many were already that one drink too far and puked and pissed as they hurled. As the night pressed, the Oompa Loompas got surlier, meaner, nastier, ruder—intimidating the smaller groups of Wallys out of footpath space, saying that Oompa Loompas had right of way and that Wallys were shit. Eventually the Oompa Loompas teased the wrong Wally who was not about to let the intimidation slide. His red and white jumper bulged from muscles underneath it. His Wally pal, who also stretched out his jumper, stood by his side, ready for whatever.

'Go on, run on to your little Wally party,' said an Oompa Loompa. 'Good girls.'

'Gate 68?' I said, cycling over. The Wally was on the very brink of kamikaze. Nobody was calling him a girl and getting away with it. 'I've taken everyone up there already. Hop on.'

The two muscle-bound Wallys jumped on, not backing down as such, just getting to where they needed to go. I cycled on with them on the back, the Oompa Loompas jeering behind, some pulling down their dungarees, mooning the muscle-bound Wallys.

Gate 68 was heaving with Wallys. They were cane-fighting out on the street, arguing with the bouncers about ID, sitting outside on the footpath puking, crying, kissing and drunk-dialing. I braked. The two

Wallys had been heavy. Muscle weighed more than fat.

I cycled on to find the Oompa Loompas stopped by cops.

'We've had complaints of unpaid bar tabs left by a rowdy stag party of Oompa Loompas,' a cop said.

'Wasn't us,' one leery Oompa Loompa said.

'Must've been some other group of Oompa Loompas,' the cop said.

'Must've been,' the Oompa Loompa said, squaring off to the sarcasm, getting right up in the cop's face. The cop radioed for assistance. This meant vanloads of cops would be arriving soon who had been cooped up all-night and itching for stuff to kick off. The leading Oompa Loompa took charge to calm things down. He took out the kitty and handed over the amount of money outstanding to a bar manager waiting in the wings then assured the cops that the belligerent and disorderly amongst them were going back to the hotel. 'Go back to the hotel, Arnold—you too, Williams,' he said. I was called over. 'Take them both up to St. Giles.'

The two naughty Oompa Loompas sat up on my backseat.

The situation satisfied the cops, and that would be the end of it, as long as the two sacrificial Oompa Loompas left.

I cycled on.

'Pigs,' shouted Arnold. Williams hiccupped agreement.

I took a left up Greek Street, forgetting it was where the Wally party was taking place. The Wallys perked up like meerkats when they saw Oompa Loompa orange.

'Look at these Muppets, everybody dressing up like Wallys,' shouted Arnold.

The Wallys moved to the edge of the path to throw the internationally recognised symbol of *wanker* at us as we passed. I gave them as wide a berth as I could.

'You're the wankers,' shouted Arnold.

I heard a loud slap. The rickshaw shook. I looked back around to see Arnold having knelt up on the backseat with a Wally beanie in his hand and a gaggle of seething Wallys giving chase. I stood up off the saddle and pedalled until my thighs burned, until my calves stung.

'Watch out,' I shouted to the Britneys, the vampires, the Bonnies and the Clydes.

'Give them back the beanie,' I shouted.

'It's my beanie now,' Arnold said.

The Wallys were impressive sprinters. One had grabbed hold of the rickshaw with one arm and was attempting to grab Arnold with the other. Another Wally swung his cane. Arnold kept both attacks at bay with deflective karate chopping. Williams was asleep.

'For fuck sake, stop looking behind and go,' Arnold shouted.

I was tempted to stop and let the Wallys have him but then I thought, no, these are my passengers and

I need to get them home. They had asked me to take them home, and that was what I was going to do.

I felt the pedal shaft bending against the thirty stone of Oompa Loompa and the pull of two Wallys. Then it snapped as I thought it would, as it had snapped on my first day with the Scotsman fare. This time I was quicker and lunged forward to avoid a testicle pounding, grabbing the steering column and hanging like a cowboy, low at the side of his horse to avoid gunfire. The Wallys climbed on board. I lost control entirely and the rickshaw slammed into the footpath. I fell off, winded by the slam of my back on the road.

The two Oompa Loompas got a thumping then the Wallys walked triumphantly back to Gate 68 with the stolen beanie. Arnold and Williams sat on the footpath edge, their big-hipped white dungarees ripped and blood-dripped. Arnold held his nose up to try and stop the flow of blood.

'Some cyclist you are,' Arnold said.

The brand of my new rickshaw was Maximus. Pedals were connected to pedal shafts that on the Maximus were moulded to the crank. The chain ran on the crank. If the pedal shaft broke, the entire crank needed replacing. I phoned Vasilly.

'I don't have the crank. You took last one before. This bullshit,' he said. 'Try Martha.'

'Who's Martha?'

'You don't know Martha? She has nice crank for you.'

I could hear Arman giggling in the background.

'Well, where can I find her?'

'Where about you is?'

'Soho Square.'

Vasilly hung up.

Martha arrived ten minutes later on her rickshaw. She was a good three inches taller than me and I was six foot. I reckoned she was about forty years old but dressed herself like an eleven-year-old Spice Girl fanatic. She was odd, not that I cared about odd, just, she was. Her cheekbones were high and her eyes sunk in behind them. Her nose had been made pointier in surgery. I had a gut feeling about something. I had only ever seen transsexuals on the telly. It wasn't like they were a dime a dozen on the streets of Ballybailte. And it didn't matter if she was a man—live and let live and all that, it was just, I wanted to know for sure.

'So you need a crank?' she asked, her vowel sounds low and deep like Johnny Cash.

'Yes. Please. If you wouldn't mind.'

'What're you staring at?'

'Nothing.'

'It's rude to stare.'

'Sorry.'

'It'll cost Vasilly sixty. Tell him. And tell him not to try and charge you for it. It's the Maximus's fault and he's the one who chose Maximus even though I told him Ecopromo. Tight Russian. And tell him to put a t-shirt on,' she said, taking a toolbox from underneath her backseat. She had giant shovel hands that tore the plastic off a brand new crank and got to work. Her fingers were fat, dirty and cut from manual work. I pretended to help by holding the handlebars steady.

I looked down. Her Adam's apple caught the light. She looked up and caught me staring again. I tried to make it seem like a ponderous stare and not an Adam's apple inspection stare.

'What?' she said.

'Just remembered something.'

'What?'

'What?'

'Did you remember?'

A zombie walked towards us from Oxford Street, in character, his legs straight, his arms held out in front of him, emitting long groaning sounds.

'That it's Halloween. I forgot,' I said, nodding towards the zombie.

'The zombie walk,' she said.

The angry pirate was back. 'Geezers, you know Leicester Square Theatre around here?' he said, this time with a destination in mind.

'I'm not a geezer,' said Martha.

He took one look at Martha and rolled his eyes. 'You're a geezer, mate.'

'Leicester Square is that way,' Martha said, pointing towards Oxford Street, the opposite direction of Leicester Square. The pirate walked towards Oxford Street.

'You English love your dressing up,' I said, regretting it. 'Not like that, I meant, fancy dress—like dressing up as Batman not a woman. I mean you are a woman. *I* think you're a woman. Doesn't matter to me and all that, whatever. I'm easy.'

Martha stopped working on the crank and looked up at me. 'Irish.'

'Yes, Martha.'

'Shut up.'

'Will do.'

'Halloween's like pushing open a cubicle door in a public toilet. For the most part it fares out fine enough. But sometimes, you uncover the horrors of humanity.'

I laughed.

'You have a Homeric laugh,' she said. 'You hear it from all the guys out on the street—big over the top laughs—trying to say *I'm OK, I'm OK, really I'm fine. Nothing wrong with us. We're just good-time blokes.*'

She reached into the toolbox for an Allen key and I stared at her breasts during the manoeuvre. His breasts. The breasts.

'You want a feel?'

'What?'

'You want to feel them?'

'No, thanks.'

'Then stop staring,' she said and fixed the new crank on. 'You think I'm a freak?'

'No. I mean. You don't have?'

'I'm a woman.'

The unworldly-yokel hole I had dug for myself was as about as deep as it was going to get but she was taking it all with a pinch of salt. 'So you don't have?'

'No, I don't have a willy.'

'So what then?'

'What then what?'

'Do you have?'

'I have what they call a vagina. Clitoris sold separately.'

Martha gave the bolts a good fastening and stood up, putting the toolbox back in her rickshaw.

'Well, thanks for fixing my crank. I really do appreciate it. And I'll tell Vasily about the t-shirt.'

'Have you broken the crank before?'

'Once.'

'You're a heavy peddler then. Lot of guys with issues are heavy peddlers.'

'What?' I said, a bit taken aback. I laughed because it was awkward. 'I don't have any issues. At all.'

'Methinks the Irishman dost protest too much. You have a girlfriend?'

'No.'

'Wife?'

'No.'

'You ever have a girlfriend?'

'I'm not gay.'

'Why don't you have a girlfriend?'

'They always broke up with me.'

'Because you're gay?'

'Because I drank.'

'Name your last girlfriend.'

'Marie.'

'How long did it last?'

'Three days.'

'That's not a girlfriend. You a closet case?'

'A closet case?'

'Guys take jobs in and around Soho sometimes, sort of testing the water before diving in. You're the only Irish guy I've ever known does it. So why?'

'It's helped me give up booze.'

'So you can get her back?'

'I was just tired of booze.'

'The other riders were speculating. They thought maybe you were a cop. I said gay.'

'Fair enough.'

'You don't go to the rider parties.'

'I'd prefer just to cycle.'

'How long've you not been drinking?'

'Two months.'

'I used to be a coke addict. Careful this job doesn't swallow you up. Get another outlet. So you wrote the letter then?'

'Yes.'

'You're an idiot.'

'Vasily liked it.'

'Vasily's an idiot.'

'Why?'

'Because the illiterate rickshaw driver gets the blame and life goes on.'

More zombies came down from Oxford Street, groaning and moaning with outstretched hands, taking pretend-bites out of normal folk. Some had been chainsawed and shot. Some had axes lodged in the back of their heads and blood running down their faces. Others had scurvy teeth with dead contact lenses inserted to give the hollow zombie look. They swamped both of our rickshaws on their way down to Old Compton Street, walking over our backseats, grabbing at us for the laugh.

'Get away from me,' said Martha, elbowing them away while she rooted around in her toolbox, took a flap of beef out of its packaging with her dirty fingers, rolled it into a tube and then chomped it back in two big bites.

'You want some?'

'No thanks. And thanks again for the crank.'

'No problem, Irish. See you around,' Martha said, hopping up on her saddle and away she pedalled. 'And don't write the Russian any more fucking letters.'

Marie & Vanessa

We woke on Sunday morning in her bedroom, naked and estranged, a pair of ducks waking from dreams in which we were swans.

She pretended to be asleep.

'This where it gets awkward?' I asked.

'Yeah,' she said, and smiled.

I kissed her on her forehead. My tongue juiced. I grabbed my boxer shorts from the floor, put them on and made for the en suite, fast. I closed the door and heard her springing up in search of clothes on the other side. I heaved over the toilet bowl and everything came up: the vodka and viscous whiskey, the Sambuca, the soupy beer, all ending with a gigantic splash. Spit drooled from my gums. I sucked from the sink's cold tap, at head height from where I knelt. The metal taste of tap soured in my mouth. I looked myself in the mirror. Someone stared back, someone older than I remembered, someone who was fucking old. My lip was cut from a punch to the mouth and there were scrapes and scratches all over my body. Niamh was in my head telling me, don't-come-back-here on repeat. I had no idea what I was going to do next and the hangover was not helping with the fear of it.

When I finally opened the bathroom door there was a half naked little girl, about seven years old, standing in front of me with a disgusted expression. She had chubby cheeks and shiny ringlets. Goldilocks in her underwear.

'Were you gettin' sick were ya?'she said.

'I was, yeah. Yeah, I was,' I said, pre-empting looking ridiculous if I tried denying it. 'Must've been bad food.'

'Me bollocks bad food, d'ya hear'm?'

'Vanessa, watch your language or you'll get a slap,' Marie said, sitting on the bed, not quite sure what to do or what to say or how to act. She had put on a pair of sweat pants, a t-shirt and a cardigan. Her clothes from the night before were off the floor and draped across a chair. The rose was gone from the bedside locker.

'The smell of beer off him but,' Vanessa said and crossed her arms at me for having her threatened with a slap, quickly forgave me and tried balancing on the tips of her toes, using my arm as support when the attempt failed.

'Wow,' I said, feeling dirty in my boxer shorts, a little girl holding my arm. 'Very good.'

'It's called en pointe. Ballet. It's hard as fuck.'

'Vanessa, I'm warning you,' Marie said, head in her hands and looking down at the carpet.

'Y'all right now?' Vanessa asked.

'Good. Thank you,' I said. Vanessa began to show me more ballet. I put both my hands over my groin and then slid one down to try cover my hairy thighs.

'Do you want some flat 7UP?' Vanessa asked.

'No thanks, thank you though,' I said, brushing past her to sit on the bed and pull a sheet over my waist. 'They're strange knickers you have on. All zig-zags on them.'

'Come on Vanessa, let...' she said and stalled, '*the man* get dressed.'

'Me dress is in your wardrobe,' Vanessa said.

'Jesus, what time is it?' Marie asked. This was serious. The game had changed.

'I dunno,' Vanessa said.

She looked at the alarm clock on the locker then leaned in to make sure it really said the time it said.

'Jesus fucking Christ. It's half ten. Where's your Granny?"

'She went to hers to get ready. We thought you were up.'

'Ah Jesus, get ready now Vanessa—we'll be late,' Marie said then grabbed an outfit in dry cleaners plastic from her wardrobe. 'Go on Vanessa, now—leave him to get dressed, get ready in your room—go on,' she said and stood at the bathroom door for a split second, took a look towards the toilet to make sure it was safe. She shut the door. The electric shower powered on.

'Do you swim?' Vanessa asked, having all the time in the world now that Mammy was in the shower.

'I do yeah, eh yeah, not very well though.'

'I have to use armbands. Christina doesn't. She can swim without armbands and won't shut up about it.'

Vanessa outstretched her arms into two wide arcs. 'It's a pirouette. You want to see me dress? It's gorgeous.' She walked over to the wardrobe, opened the bottom drawer to use it as a step-up to the hangers, unhooked a big white fluffy ball and threw it onto the bed then jumped down off the drawer, landing badly.

'Mind yourself,' I said.

'I'm grand. Relax,' Vanessa said, picking herself up off the ground.

'You getting married?' I asked, nodding my broken head at the big white fluffy dress.

'It's me first Holy Communion today. I've to do a readin' and eat a bit of Jesus and all that. Did you use a condom?'

'What?'

'I'd like a baby sister.'

'Jesus,' I said and pressed all ten fingers into my head, hard.

'Ah look, look, they're right under your feet there, would y'look,' Vanessa said, pointing out my trousers. I reached down to pick them up and the buzzing head returned, bile oozing up my throat.

'You look like trampled shite,' Vanessa said, got her dress out of my vomiting radius and laid it on the ground, a chiffon, satin and lace embroidered ball of white floral pattern that materialized in my broken head as some sort of hole in the universe. She stepped inside it, left foot first then the right and pulled it up and around her, vanishing inside the white except for her head.

'Do me zip up will ya?'

She walked over, presenting me with her back. I took the zip and pulled it up quickly, catching the material in the rung.

'Careful.'

I took it again and poked out the material from the rung, proceeding to pull it up gently, looking away as I did so, ready to leap up and declare my innocence should authorities burst through the door.

'Dad has me tiara outside. Dad! Bring in the tiara, Dad!' Vanessa shouted out to the hallway. Cold pins and needles shot through my face and fingertips. My heart forgot to beat. The films were wrong—life did not flash before your eyes in the final moments. Death did. And it was a violent one where nobody could hear me scream, at the hands of Dad and all of his North Dublin inner-city cronies. There were wrenches and vices and blowtorches and when I begged them to just finish him off they all laughed and singed my eyeballs with cigarettes.

But the bedroom door stayed shut.

'He must be doing his weights,' Vanessa said.

'I better head off,' I said, frantically searching for my shoes, already wondering about a drainpipe down to the street.

'Relax, I'm only playing. He left us. That's why she's sad. Where are you from, the country?' Vanessa said, smiling to herself, affixing her bag over her shoulders and taking out beaded white gloves, struggling her hands into them. The shower switched off.

'You were messing with me?' I asked, looking around for leftover booze from the night before to calm my nerves. There was wine on the floor. I unscrewed the top and slugged.

'Do you drink a lot?'

'Yes,' I said. 'I do.'

'I don't like her drinking. She only does it when she's sad. She never takes showers when she's the only one in the house. Isn't that weird? What do you think of veils?'

'Veils?'

'The ones over your face that you wear for weddings and maybe Holy Communions. Veils—white veils,' said Vanessa attempting another demi-plié in the dress.

'What do *you* think of them?'

Vanessa looked around to make sure the coast was clear for some serious swearing.

'I fuckin' hate them,' she said and palmed down the bodice, reached her head back as far as she could manage so as to make sure everything was in order. 'Rotten things they are. It's a Communion. What do you need a veil for?'

'Does Christina have a veil?'

'Won't shut up about it,' said Vanessa.

'Tiaras are the way forward I think,' I said. 'In my opinion. To hell with veils.'

'So what does your Mammy think of you drinking?'

'My Mam died,' I said. 'But I have a sister who doesn't like it.'

'Good. What's her name?'

'Niamh.'

'I like Niamh then.'

Vanessa took her eyes off me for a split second and I pulled up my trousers underneath the sheet. She heard the movement and turned back around, staring unashamedly, trying to catch one last glimpse of my zigzagged boxer shorts. I pulled out the bit of sheet that had been tucked inside my trousers with the manoeuvre, stood up and swayed a tad from the blood rush to the head. I found my t-shirt and put it on, a sock and put that on, a shoe then the other sock then found the second shoe.

'Right,' I said, looking at her looking at me.

'What's your job?'

'I'm a sparky. I wire houses and factories for electricity, make sure it all has power and lights and all that sort of thing. Yeah—electrician.'

'You make much cash?'

'Not these days. Work's a bit scarce actually,' I said and waited for her to ask another question but she did not. Instead she tucked her bottom lip beneath the top one, folding her arms at the same time.

'Right, right, Communion,' I said and reached for my wallet in my back pocket. I found a two twenties and a fiver, the last bit of money I had. I pinched the fiver inside the wallet and looked at her looking at them. I took out a twenty and gave it over.

'Cheers,' she said, slipping it inside her bag. 'What about the rest?'

'You want the rest, too?'

'What do you need it for?'

I handed it all over. She slipped the forty-five inside her bag. 'You want the wallet and all?'

'No. I've a purse.'

I finished off the wine.

'You'd want to stop drinking so much.'

'I know.'

'Granny saw you coming in last night. She said you had an arsehole face.'

The bathroom door opened and Marie came out dressed in a coral pants suit and white blouse, her hair cleaned, her face scrubbed, teeth brushed and rinsed twice with mouthwash. She looked rejuvenated and put a spring in her step to show it. She spotted the empty wine bottle in my hand. I tried to hide it pathetically. She threw her eyes to heaven then rushed about the room to show she was busy, to show I had to skedaddle. She plugged in the hairdryer and began shaking it, running it through wet strands of her hair.

'Vanessa, are you ready?'

'I've to put my socks and shoes on.'

'Well go do it will you, or we'll be late.'

Vanessa went to her room. I stood up and shifted weight from one foot to the other. She looked at me in the reflection of the dresser's mirror and shook the hairdryer harder through her hair.

'Look,' Marie said. 'I went off the rails a bit. Her father fucked off and I went, yeah, just off the rails a bit. I'm not like that. I don't act like that.'

'That's fine,' I said.

'What I'm saying is, I like you, I do. But, this isn't going to work.'

'I'm trying to sort myself out.'

'Well, sort it. Come back when it's all good enough for you the way it is. I'm sorry. Look, I've heard all this before. With her father. I'm not putting her through it. Around and around. It's bollocks. It's OK for men to go off and have their little existential crises but I have responsibilities—ballet and fuckin' poxy Communions and Christ, I'm not swapping one for another just as bad. I'm sorry.'

'I'll head off, get out of your way.'

'OK,' she said. 'Any of the buses at the end of the road will take you into town.'

'Brilliant. Good luck with it.'

'What?' she said, the noise of the dryer getting the better of the conversation. She switched it off and turned around to look at me, making sure not to smile but not to frown either. Neutral, she was keeping it neutral.

'I just said—good luck with the Communion. She's a nice kid. She's funny.'

'Thanks,' she said. 'If I could stop her swearing.'

'It's a phase with them, isn't it?' I said.

'She's just doing it to get noticed.'

'Well, I think you have the next big ballerina on your hands there. I'll be watching out for her,' I said finally, waiting, suggesting she could maybe say something instead.

'Bye now, Joe,' she said, switched the hairdryer back on and got back to business on the strands still wet. I turned. She got on with drying. I hurried down the stairs and opened the front door then closed it behind me. The rain had started and the puddles collected. Drops dripped from the locked bicycles and that was it really. A day for the ducks. The houses snoozed on, curtains still drawn. The cars stayed parked, nobody to work, nobody for a jog, nobody venturing out for fresh orange juice or breakfast rolls. Nobody could even look at food, a time fit for only paracetemol and maybe a hammer over the head to knock them out. I looked up at the bedroom window and wanted back inside.

'It'll be fine,' Vanessa said out through the letterbox.

'Thanks.'

'What're you going to do, now?'

'Maybe go to London.'

'You have any money?'

'No.'

'Make money. Girls like that.'

'Do they, yeah?'

'Here,' she said and put the forty-five out through the letterbox. 'For your ticket.'

'Thanks,' I said. 'I'll pay you back.'

'I think she likes you. But like she said, she needs someone stable and you're a

fuckin' mess.'

'You don't think I have an arsehole face?'

'You do. But that's OK. It's what's on the inside that counts.'

'Yeah?'

'No. It's just what I say to Christina. She's an ugly little bitch.'

MONEY HUNGRY

I'd chase money, make big bags of the stuff and wave it around, maybe invest in property, be the first rickshaw rider in history to be launched onto the stock market, get a big vault and swim in all my money like Scrooge McDuck. The whole city was obsessed with it. You could see it in people's walk to work—left, money, right, money, left, money. It was an agenda, a raison d'être. They must've been doing it for something—not to be happy—*money can't make you happy*, they say—*you can't take it with you*. But the car, the house, the holiday—to have the most, maybe meant you were the best. That's why Arman showed his off in front of the newbies. Money was status. Fuck it, I'd chase money, make big bags of the stuff and be envied by the other riders, feed off their jealousy.

There must've been something in it.

'Soho,' explained the tour guide at my side, 'was the hunt's cry when it cantered across the countryside in chase of the fox. It meant, get-out-of-the-bloody-way basically and when the peasants who lived around here heard it, they found shelter at the side of the fields or risked a trampling by Henry the Eighth and his horses. The hunt did not stop. This was back a thousand years ago when all of these streets and buildings did not exist. When this was all countryside. So when they had to come up with a name for it, they called it *Soho*, leaving it cry onto itself, warning itself out of its own hurtling path.'

The tourists in the guide's group shouted *Soho* for the laugh as they moved on.

From around the corner of Dean Street came Stink carrying a plastic bag full of ink cartridges for a printer.

'Can I have the rest of that delicious libation you are consuming currently, Irish?'

I handed over the energy drink I was holding. He smashed it back, a good portion of it dribbling down his front.

'You want to buy ink cartridges?

'No thanks.'

'Bike lights?'

'No.'

'How's the pedal trade then?'

'I've decided to make loads of money.'

'I can show you how to make big money—big money.'

'I know about strip clubs.'

'Not strip clubs—no, no, not strip clubs. Thirty-five quid a head—a pox on them. Getting Irish guys there who tremble on seeing the place and just run off. Or getting ripped off by the bouncers? No Irish, no. I know a place for one-fifty a head. I know places for a grand a head.'

'Where?'

'Give me fifty of your pounds and I shall divulge.'

'I'll find out without having to pay fifty quid.'

'Go right ahead,' he said, scurrying off into the crowd and out of sight.

I made for Martha. The Bangladeshis and Turks saw her as a mythological creature, alerting themselves in a frenzy when they saw her coming, hopping over one another to throw questions at her as though she were a portal to God—*Martha, where you go tonight? Hey Martha, will be good night tonight?* She trawled Rupert and Brewer, a rainbow-coloured corner of Soho full of high-pitched excitement, baby oil and tank-top.

'To what do I owe the pleasure, Irish?' Martha said when I pulled up behind her. She had eyes in the back of her head.

'You know Stink?'

'What's he stolen off you?'

'Nothing. He was just saying there're places that pay one-fifty-a-head commission. You know those places?'

Martha pointed a dirty finger at me, the question having pissed her off and she rolled up a sleeve to show it. 'I'll tell you what I tell everyone—I'm a rickshaw rider. Not a pimp. And I don't bring people to those places. I don't agree with it.'

'It's brothels that he's talking about then?'

'After Parties.'

'But they're all over here.'

'It's not the walk-ups. It's private houses. And I wouldn't tell you even if I knew.'

An engine revved behind us and I was jolted from my saddle. I wound up on the floor of the backseat, shocked, bruised and winded.

'Get out of the fuckin' way you cretin,' someone shouted.

I looked up to see a cabbie hanging out his window.

Martha reached under her backseat to produce a thick chain with a fuck-off lock attached to the end.

'What was that?' she asked the cabbie who was now silent and regretful with nowhere to go. He couldn't reverse. He couldn't drive forwards. He was at the mercy of Martha who swung the chain and brought the lock down perfectly on his bonnet. It was four hundred pounds damage just like that. 'What was that?' she said again. She wasn't stopping. She walked around the side and swung the lock down on his windscreen, then on his door panel then on his roof. She was totalling his cab. Everybody around was acting like it was just another thing. 'What was that?' she kept saying and the cabbie only sat there, not leaving the safety of his cab, just saying 'Sorry, I'm sorry, OK? I'm sorry!'

'This is your letter at work, Irish,' she called after me as I cycled on.

The only other girl rider was Norwegian. Her name was Gunda and she was the real deal, rolling by me at that very moment.

'Hey, Irish.'

'Hey, Gunda. Martha's totalling a cab back there.'

'She does it every now and then.'

Gunda made a killing up outside Candy bar. The lesbians loved her and took rides with her even when they didn't want to go anywhere. She got guys to strip clubs as well as any rider and smiled when the guys asked was she *doin any strippin* on the way. However, should an over-zealous strip club punter pinch her bottom, woe be-fucking-tide them. She would lunge into the backseat with her rickshaw still rolling, going straight for the throat of the pincher, intent on ripping out his larynx. Even though every rider would want to come to her rescue, it was the pincher who they ended up rescuing.

'Hey, Gunda, you know about After Parties?'

'Why? You not getting any action, Irish?' she said as she cycled away.

I cycled down to Windmill Street and parked beside the riders there who perpetually parked beside the open street-urinals. Guys pissed beside them all night long and they weren't bothered by it in the slightest. It was one of their rickshaws that had been photographed by *The Evening Standard* mangled up and crunched beneath a bus.

They spoke to each other about how long until the claim money arrived. I would see them up on

Oxford Street, in the places where the street narrowed so as to allow for traffic light islands. This was where the traffic bottlenecked into one very narrow lane with room for only one vehicle between the curbing. They would overtake a double-decker bus right before the narrowing, holding it up to a snails pace. They hoped for the right bus driver, the type of guy who took it personally, who was having a bad day, who would keep his foot on the accelerator and jam the rickshaw against the curbing. This broke the differential in half. It sometimes even dragged the entire thing underneath. These guys though, jumped off the rickshaw and onto the footpath in the nick of time. They used a solicitor's firm up in Tottenham to lodge a claim for the cost of the rickshaw. They had a constant stream of cheques coming in from London Bus settling out of court, compensating for destroyed rickshaws, two grand a pop. They had Martha fix up the rickshaws and repair the differential for five hundred.

They were the lummoxes of the rickshaw world, unemployable, beer-bellied and chain-smoking. They refused tourists who wanted small rides around Piccadilly or down to Leicester Square. They studied racing form and made illegible scribbles in the margins, all part of their formula to try and reconfigure the force times distance moved equation.

'Quiet night,' I said to a guy in a big coat, hands in his pockets, sitting in his own backseat.

'And?' he said.

'Just saying—not much going on.'

He spotted a pair of tall, drunken lads leaving the table-dancing club up the street, talking pussy.

'Company tonight, fellas? Some girls? Full service.'

They ignored him and kept on walking.

'That for the one-fifty-a-head place?' I asked.

'Piss off,' he said, looking at me like I just had sex with his sister. He took out his racing form and got scribbling.

I cycled on, meeting Bertie on his American-themed rickshaw. He was parked outside the Prince Edward. The idea of the American theme was to attract American tourists. He was Italian, about fifty years old. He liked a gamble but had a strict one bet a day policy. Ten pounds—that was it. He had been married to an Irish woman who left him and took everything when it had gotten out of hand. He had bet away holiday funds, got a second chance, then a third chance and then bet away the mortgage repayments.

'Her father was a big gambler, too,' he had said. 'Lost their house. So she couldn't go through it all again. I understand. A nice woman.'

Bertie wore knee high shorts like an old-fashioned toddler in the comics. Together with a pirate bandana, coke-bottle glasses that magnified his eyeballs three times as big, and his multitude of Hawaiian shirts, he was a sight to behold outside the theatres as the crowd burst. He sang *Hakuna Matata* or *Mamma*

Mia at the top of his voice, doing well, attracting those who wanted the fun to keep going, chasing the good time even though the show was over.

'You're too good to be true, darling, I can't take my eyes from you, yea? I need you on my rickshaw, baby,' Bertie said to the crowd.

'You know Stink, Bertie?'

'Yes, I know this bastard. He stole my rickshaw once. I caught him trying to sell it down on Trafalgar for twenty pounds. He was rickshaw rider long time ago. He make very good money and bought a limo. So then, he go out to Heathrow and wait for the Arabs. He charge them thousand pound to go into Knightsbridge or Park lane. And Arab pay—they have billions. They don't care about thousands. But BBC catch him. They put him on television with a big stupid face. Then police throw him in jail. He like the stuff now.' Bertie pointed to the veins in the underside of his arm, pretending to inject one with a needle.

'He showed me the place you can bring fares for one-fifty-a-head. The After Party. Martha says she doesn't agree with it.'

'I know what she think, and I don't see Martha doing protests outside the place. So she can go to Hell. I have to eat. Don't tell her I said this.'

'Stink was saying it's just up there a bit,' I said, pointing north then west, 'but I forget where exactly he said.'

The ploy had great big bells on it and Bertie had heard it coming from miles off.

'I can't tell you, Irishman. You bring me some customer. We halve them. Then I show you, OK?'

He looked like the kid with all the chocolate. That was why Bertie gambled. He liked to be the guy in the know with the cash to back it up. He loved being a step ahead of everyone else. The successful riders like Bertie learned from the people on the street. They watched the leaflet distributers, the charity muggers, the zany *Big Issue* sellers, the panhandlers, the heroin addicts, the homeless, the street sketchers, the human signs, the event promoters, the advertising and took tactic from it all. They learned from the past, from initiations gone awry and situational stalemates and made sure they had the right answer the next time. They knew the angles to play for different types of tips—pretend to be a poor student trying to make a better life if the customers were educated, pretend to be a poor grafter trying to make enough money for a few pints if the customers had trades. They learned to know where people wanted to go just by the direction they were walking and the clothes they were wearing, playing the cheeky scallywag, the entertainer, sharp with quips and comebacks.

I looked around and Stink was at my side, the ink cartridges nowhere to be seen.

'Finished the investigation, Sherlock?' he said.

'I heard you were a rider once upon a time, Stink.'

'Bertie the old gambaholic telling tales again, then? Come on, Irish. I need my medicine. Come,

come then— give me forty of your pounds and I'll tell you. Give me forty, there's a good lad.'

'I'll need you to show me.'

'I ain't goin there, no can do. Can't do it. I owe the Russians some pounds.'

'How do I know you won't just tell me a random address and I show up to some old lady's house with six randy lager-louts?'

'Why would I, fella? When I'm being paid to give you the right address? Why

would I do it?' He was clawing fingernails into his neck and getting itchy and pissed off at having to sell it to me. 'Give me twenty.'

I took a twenty out of my pocket and handed it over. Stink looked at it, twitching and itching and hurting, holding his groin like he was going to piss himself.

'7 Brandwell Gardens. Bell's at the back entrance,' he said, turned and ran down the street grinding his teeth, gripping the twenty hard in charge, hot on the heels of his quarry.

'Out of the way,' he was shouting. 'Out of the bloody way.'

THE PAST

Icalled him Roland because it fit for a fruitcake. I would see him tart-carding the phone boxes down in Westminster and Victoria. It was dominatrix tart-cards promising pain and torture to attract the politicians. Running the country required your arse whipped raw while being called a dirty, little bitch every now and then. Roland would arrive outside Victoria Station, tart-card the phone box and then take exactly sixteen steps. If a woman passed on the sixteenth step, he would say—'Excuse me, would you like to go for a drink with me?'

If the propositioned ignored him, which was always the case, he would turn and walk back the sixteen steps to the spot he had started from and ask again—'Excuse me, would you like to go for a drink with me?'

He did that every evening, back and forth the sixteen steps from 6pm to 7pm, giving himself dogs abuse all the way home, calling himself stupid then reassuring himself that she *will* show, that tomorrow he *will* meet her.

I had begun talking to myself, too—sarcastic at first, to entertain fares because they thought guys must be mad in the first place to even consider the job. I would weave in and out through traffic with inches to spare before collisions, and people would whisper in the backseat about how you would want your head checked to ride a rickshaw.

Talking to myself met an expectation.

It was also good for practicing quips and retorts, to counter people's reasons for not riding on the rickshaw. It just took time and practice because more or less, everybody said the same thing. I took the rejection, word for word, stole away with it for hours, rolled it over and over again in my head, figured every possible permutation. I said it aloud as I pedalled—*No thanks mate, we got legs.*

No thanks mate, we got legs.

No thanks mate, we got legs.

I turned it into a mantra, relived the story until eventually I caught it square on—*They don't have a map though.*

'We got legs, mate,' a man would say on the side of the street later.

'Yes but the legs don't have a map,' I'd say and he would walk on trying to find his destination to spite me.

I would steal away with it again, *we got legs, mate* rolling over in my head, pedalling through traffic, saying *we got legs, mate, we got legs, mate, we got legs, mate.* I would take offense, throw back a *how-dare-you* at myself, call myself a cretin, tell myself to just fuck-off or say that I had no cash on me, sorry. I would have it all on the tip of my tongue and wait for *we-got-legs* to come around again as it inevitably did.

'No thanks, darling, we got legs,' a woman would say.

'And what fine legs they are, madam. They would look fabulous sitting up in my backseat don't you think? I tell you what, you rest them a minute, I'll get them to where they need to go. It just so happens I'm doing a two-for-one special on gorgeous legs.'

It was learning from the past.

The money though, wasn't coming quickly enough. There was still too much sitting around, haggling, arguing over price, stalemates. It was the found that were the problem, and the capable, the map-readers, the pre-planners.

Our grandfather had once told Niamh and I a story of when he was a boy during the Second World War. He lived in Ballybailte, which was even smaller back then, during days when people churned their own butter. He was in the town square with *his* father, our great grandfather. They stood watching another man from the town on a ladder, smearing all the street names away with wet cement. A crowd formed around the man as he went, helping with his ladder and holding his bucket. Our grandfather said he took it in turns with other boys from the town to hold the man's trowel in between street names.

'This'll cod them,' the man said as he smeared over the Church Street plaque.

The crowd went out the Ballybeggan road and pulled all the signposts out of the ground like carrots. Places were no longer seven miles that way or two miles the other way. They walked out the Ballyhale road and did the same.

I was on Oxford Circus at the stair-mouth to one of its tube exits. The crowd coming out from it surrounded the public map to get a bearing. There were four of these maps on the south side of the Circus and four on the north side. They were state of the art, colour-coordinated, location-finding apparatuses. They pointed arrows to Piccadilly Circus, east to Marylebone, west to Fitzrovia and north to Regent's Park. They detailed everything within a fifteen-minute walking radius and beneath this again, was the five-minute walking radius map, an enhanced version that put the immediate surrounding streets into high definition. Every building had its name tagged on it. Everything was on there—Hanover Square, the London Palladium, the Langham, the London College of Fashion. Then, to add insult to injury, there were was the big red dot giving the whole game way in the centre of each—*YOU ARE HERE.* The maps gave away the past and told the future. There was just no competing with their informative nature. They gave people directions and goals and targets. Everyone had little know-where-we're-going grins and brisk walks. I was superfluous to these found people because of these maps.

My phone started to ring. It was Niamh. I let it ring out. I needed to get going.

It was one minute past six o'clock. The graffiti removals units were officially off for the weekend.

I put on a baseball cap and took out from underneath the backseat one of the spray cans I had bought earlier. I ran over to the first monster-map and sprayed left to right, right to left in one long line, working my way down one side. Oxford Street and Regent Street were both wiped off the face of the earth. Arrows, street indexes and direction were a thing of The Past. One woman tried to get one last look at where Carnaby Street was before it vanished. Others gave some questioning expressions, borderline angry but soon tired of caring and walked on. I went around the other side and did the same until the whole thing was a block of red sticking up out of the footpath. I ran across the Circus and did the same to the second monster-map then to the third, then the fourth. It took 3 cans of red to do the four of them—one big red dot—*YOU ARE HERE.* That was all the information there was now, not where they had come from or where they were going—just where they were at that very moment—there. I had blindfolded the whole place. A rickshaw rider relied on a deceitful slant on things anyway—man-eating strip clubs and false information—this was just taking it one step further.

'What's with the maps?' Bertie said, rolling to my side then noticed my red hands. 'You'll get in big, big trouble for this, Irish. These people call cops. The CCTV is everywhere. They are going to lock you up, man.'

'The cops just refer it to the graffiti removal units. They close at six. They're only allowed weekend overtime if it's racist or offensive. This is just red.'

Bertie took a look around at the panicked faces and started to do the math. The city-break couples were stressing out. The restaurant goers were late for their booking and the Maître D's were calling, telling them their table would be given away in ten minutes. Curtain-up was in an hour and the theatre crowd had to get to the other side of Covent Garden, and collect the tickets, and try to grab something quick to eat.

'So, the maps will be out all weekend here?' he said.

'Just don't go telling everyone.'

Bertie fixed up his fingerless gloves with his teeth and made his bandana good and tight at the back.

'Irish, this is good for business. And when they lock you up, I will have it all.'

'Excuse me, I have one question,' said a man, his girlfriend behind him. She adjusted her heels because her feet were sore from walking.

Bingo.

'I live in London, so I know— OK?' the man said and pointed at our rickshaws to make sure we knew he knew.

'Know what?' Bertie asked.

'That it's a con,' he said, 'taking people around the corner and charging them twenty quid.'

'It's not a con,' Bertie said. 'I have never conned in my life.'

'But look, I live in London, OK?'

'OK,' said Bertie.

'OK,' I said.

'Piccadilly Circus is that way, right?' he said, pointing up Oxford Street towards Marble Arch. He waited for us to automatically point out the true direction of Piccadilly Circus but our hands stayed on our handlebars and our eyes stayed on him.

'Nope,' I said.

'No, it is not,' said Bertie.

'The maps all got cunted,' he said.

'It's the latest Banksy,' I said.

'Really?'

'The papers have just been around photographing it. It's called, *YOU ARE HERE*, apparently. To remind people that it's only when we are lost that we can start to truly find ourselves. Says Banksy anyway.'

'I like it,' Bertie said.

'It's OK,' said the guy taking out his phone to get a picture of it. 'It's the new Banksy, sweetheart,' he said to his girlfriend. 'Like an installation. Called, what is it?'

'You are here,' I said.

'You are here,' repeated the guy. 'Sort of makes you think, doesn't it?' His girlfriend shrugged. 'So how much to Piccadilly?'

'Ten,' I said then coughed to replace the purposely unsaid, *each*.

So there was our grandfather, in Ballybailte with no signs pointing to anywhere anymore. It had not dawned on him to ask *why* the man smeared all the street names away with wet cement and why the crowd pulled up all the signposts until he was walking home with our great grandfather later that evening. Our great grandfather said it was because German spies were being dropped into Ireland and were making their way into England to spy on the English. But when they arrived, they weren't going to know where the hell they were going because there was not going to be any signs or street names to tell them.

MOTHS

Two glamorous ladies accompanied by two refined gentlemen stepped out of a bar and into the cold.

'Inside there's rules,' Martha had told me. 'Like gents must remove their hats and all that bollocks. No name-dropping and gents may not approach ladies. If they do, ladies are obligated to lift their chins and ignore the conversation. So the gents order these big buckets of champagne and wait for ladies to come to them.'

The gent's eagerness for a cab had *nightcap back at the hotel* written all over it. One of them waved me away with an expression of annoyance for even being thought of as rickshaw clientele.

Two young lads with tans, tight haircuts and tighter t-shirts passed. They were personal trainers or topless waiters and looked like what the two refined gentlemen might have looked like twenty years earlier. The gentlemen didn't notice them but the bored and shivering ladies certainly did. One of them asked one of the young lads for a light. Neither of the lads smoked but they stopped to have a chat anyway, acting cool and suave, used to such female attention.

The gentlemen waited on the edge of the foot-path for a cab, whispering about who would take the brunette.

The young lads made a gesture to their destina-tion, a cool and suave place no doubt, for beautiful people only.

'Why not?' said one of the ladies and made to walk away with the lads like it was nothing.

'Oi,' a gentlemen said.

'Thanks for the drinks,' the blonde shouted back, a young lad's hand around her waist.

The two refined gentleman were having none of it and pursued.

'Oi, we spent a lot of money in there tonight,' said the second gentleman.

The young lads stopped and squared up and everyone charged everyone else with being bang-out-of-order. The girls joined hands, fluttered their arms and pulled each other away from all of the testosterone.

'Rickshaw,' the blonde shouted.

'Rickshaw,' the brunette agreed, waving their arms at me, both of them hysterical at the thoughts of escaping in a rickshaw. They girls hopped on. The young lads tried to follow but the girls pressed at their chests and gave smiles to say that it would have to wait for another night.

'Where to?' I asked.

'Just drive, drive, drive,' said the blonde.

'He cycles.'

'Cycle, cycle, cycle, then,' the blonde corrected.

I looked back and saw the two gentlemen at the side of the footpath, watching their hopes and dreams get carried away down Piccadilly on the backseat of a rickshaw. They were a deflated pair of bastards now, stranded and miserable. They went back into the bar to drown their sorrows and talk the could-have-been.

The young lads though, chased the rickshaw, still clinging to some sort of hope, reaching at the frame, trying to step a foot inside until we reached Piccadilly Circus and melted into heavy traffic. The wall of light was a beast. It glowed like a trillion tellies and burned the air around. I looked back and found them allowing the light to shine on their faces like they were charging, their eyes closed, gulping down the phosphorescence and radiation, the liquid crystal diodes, the rays of curling, spiralling beams, the LED's, the twinkling flashes—dazzled and numbed by the brilliance—light-stoned.

I circled the Circus.

'Where to?' I said.

'Euston,' they shouted back. 'We can't make him cycle to Euston—He's alright—You alright? —Yeah, he's alright—Euston.'

I turned, curving north on Regent Street, the light of Piccadilly Circus fading behind us like a setting sun. It got colder. The girls ran out of chat. Some lads were walking beside us and the girls laughed loudly for no reason. The lads looked and the girls *yoo-hoo*ed them, trickled their fingers, tilted their heads and smiled up to their gaze.

'I like them tight jeans,' said the brunette to one.

'Room on that for us?' the lads asked, starting a gallop behind. The girls giggled.

'You's wanna come to a party, ladies?'

'We'll meet you there,' the girls laughed.

The lads kept up the brisk jog until I turned right at Oxford Circus. A blasting winter wind pushed back the rickshaw and I sat up off the saddle to fight against it. It was a bitch. Crowds lined up with burgers at bus stops or tried to flag down cabs. Birthday Boys shouted—'Back to my hotel. Someone, please.'

The city darkened at the end of Oxford Street. Lights rinsed down to amber. Shuttered-up businesses and bolted over doors took over from the neon and sparkle. The cars passed fast, their windows wound closed. Any pedestrians were now determined walkers, coat collars zipped high to the wind and headphones wrapped around their ears.

'I'm going to phone him,' said the brunette. She rooted through her purse and there was a quiet until whoever *he* was, answered.

'Tosser,' the brunette said straight-off. 'I come all the way down to London and you don't show. You're injured—so what do you need to go to the game for if you're injured?'

He told her.

'That's ridiculous. Do you hear yourself? You'll be sitting on a bench.'

He justified.

'Well tell your stupid gaffer to fuck himself.'

He said something else.

'No,' said the brunette and hung up.

'What was he banging on about?' asked the blonde.

'Usual shit,' said the brunette. 'Don't know why I bother with him.'

And then there was nothing but quiet. Headlights whipped past, taking their lights away with them fast, their taillight-reds insulting to the girls.

They began to tut, bored.

I changed to a higher gear to meet the incline of the street, the crunching of sprocket and chain-rings ground out awkward and uncomfortable sounds.

'Are you really cycling all of this?'

I looked back at them. They both jumped from the glossy page, perfumed, polished, airbrushed, preened, waxed, plucked and affixed, nails glued, breasts implanted—legs, tums and bums all worked— hair extended and teeth lasered.

'How much money you make on this then?' asked the brunette.

'Don't know,' I said. 'Thousands.'

'This is our hotel,' they said.

'One sec, girls. I'll pull onto the path,' I said, getting off and pulling the rickshaw up and onto the footpath.

The brunette pinched the blonde on the hip and whispered something into her ear. The blonde giggled.

'You want to come up?' the brunette asked.

I told myself I wanted to make money, remember. Swim around in it like Scrooge McDuck did. But I was actually thinking of the two poor bastards back down on Dover Street who could still have been around, wanting a lift home. I thought about maybe going back down there and trying to find them.

'I have no lock for the rickshaw. And I guess I need to keep going—busy and all that tonight.'

They let my answer hang, analysing it, wondering what to do about it, looking truly baffled. Then offended. They eventually asked each other if they had any cash. Neither had.

'We didn't bring out cash with us.'

'You went out in Mayfair on a Saturday night and didn't bring out any cash with you?'

They smiled at one another like I knew nothing about the world.

'I have cash in the room,' said the brunette. 'Look, we'll leave my heels with you, they're worth a grand—believe me I'll be coming back for'em.'

'Don't worry about it,' I said. I thought of only pedalling, of getting going, of cycling on, imagining gunning down Wellington Street, braking the back wheels so that I'd naturally skid to meet the Strand, taking the hill down to Trafalgar and then zooming down Whitehall, muscles burning, pistons turning.

'No, no, you'll get your money,' the brunette said.

'I really don't mind,' I said. It was getting weird.

'I'll just stay here and wait for you, babes,' the blonde said.

'I'll just be a minute,' the brunette said. She got off the rickshaw and crossed the road to the hotel.

'What was your name?' the blonde asked.

'Irish.'

'My parents are from Ireland,' she said. 'County Cork. They make sure I say I'm Irish, always telling me just because I was born in a stable don't make me a horse.'

'That's a good one.'

A gust came thumping down Euston Road.

'I have a blanket if you want it?' I said, reaching in beside her to the back compartment, taking out the blanket and handing it to her. 'You're nice,' she said. 'A gentleman.'

'No, I'm not.'

'Yes, you are. I want a man like you.'

'What do you do?'

'I'm a model,' she said, looking down at her breasts. 'I've done page three and all that—lads mags—that sort of thing. I'm not a prostitute you know.'

'I didn't say you were.'

'I have a son.'

'That's fantastic,' I said, up against the ropes and not knowing how in the hell I got there.

'I do what I do for him, so that he can have it better.'

111

The silence slapped me in the face and for longest time I could not stop it or break through it.

'I know you don't think I'm a prostitute,' she said. 'You're a gentleman. You didn't even try to look up my skirt when you were getting the blanket.'

'I'm really not a gentleman,' I said. 'You can ask anyone.'

'You didn't come up.'

'I don't have a lock that's all.'

'Sit in here with me.'

My legs were agitated. They were not pedalling and so the lactic acid was building in their joints. It felt like they were rusting up.

I wanted to get going. 'Look, don't worry about the money,' I said. 'I was happy to do it, no problem.'

'God, what's wrong with you? She'll be back in a minute then you can ride away on your little bike, Jesus Christ. I'm not just a big set of tits. My name's Briana in case you cared. I do yoga on Wednesdays and I collect my son from school everyday.'

Briana moved her hand out to mine and pulled me inside the backseat then kissed me on the ear, biting on the lobe ever so gently, breathing through her nose heavy.

'Just come up with me,' she said.

The brunette appeared at the side of the rickshaw with a man on her arm looking tall and rugby. They were laughing and shouting, whooshing and singing and shouting.

'You said limousine,' said the rugby-looking man.

'This *is* a limo, here you go, darling,' said the brunette, handing me three twenties. 'Thanks for waiting.'

'Thanks,' I said.

'Babes, this is Mike. And inside is his friend, Darren. And they have a *big* bottle of champagne ready for us inside in the bar.'

The brunette gave a silent nod to Briana that Darren was not too shabby. Briana took the blanket from her lap and helped herself out of the backseat then the trio skipped across the Euston Road towards the neon glow of the hotel sign, Mike in the middle, the blonde and the brunette locking arms with him on each side, headlights slowing down to light their way.

After Party

I found the pair of refined gentlemen, sitting on a window ledge down on Dover Street after the bar had closed, throwing thoughtful looks into space, roughened by the cold.

'Need a lift home, gents?'

'Fuck off,' one said.

'Where'd you bring the girls?' the other asked.

'Back to their hotel.'

'He could bring us up there—give it one last go.'

'They're with Mike and Darren,' I said. 'And a big bottle of champagne.'

'For fuck sake,' they both said.

'Where else is open?'

'I could probably introduce you gentlemen to some ladies if you like?'

'Could you now?'

'I could.'

'What kind of ladies?'

'Pleasing ladies,' I said.

'We're fine. I don't think my wife would appreciate me dipping off to the scrubbers while I'm down here.'

'Or mine,' the other said.

'Of course not,' I said sarcastically, implying they keep their bullshit for when they got home. 'But there's drinks there and everywhere around here's closing now. There's no obligation.'

'So, if you were to take us there—how long would it take?'

'Ten minutes. Maybe fifteen.'

'We'll take a look.'

'What harm? We'll take a look,' said the other. 'Is there a place where we could stop to buy a bottle of beer for the spin? And a cash machine?'

The gents got on board and I got pedalling. They were no pair of ballerinas. I dug deep to lug their weight, my hamstrings and quad muscles getting a good burn. I clicked the gears lower for extra hardship to take my mind off the *pleasing* ladies remark. *Jesus.*

The streets turned into one long road, the West End somewhere behind us, no buskers or giddy crowds going from pub to club, no bright signs for musical of the decade, no lagered-up lads. There was only me on the rickshaw, pulling the two gents to a place where they would meet two very pleasing ladies. Five-storied Victorian houses rolled by, kids all tucked up inside, bikes locked to the railings outside,

Rice Krispie boxes flattened and wrapped up in piles for cardboard-recycling.

The house was like all the others. There were no X's in big red neon out front, no girls lounging outside in revealing mini-skirts, rubbish burning in barrels or security guards with German Shepherds. It was just a nice house like all the others with a gravel driveway. A rickshaw was parked up at the side. I braked behind it and hopped off the saddle. The wheels sank down into the gravel, stuck.

'I'll bring you around to the back,' I said.

I walked on and they followed behind me like it was their first day at school and I was their mother. Sure enough, there was a backdoor around the corner with a bell. Stink was true to his word so far.

'It's nippy enough,' said a gent.

'Nippy all right,' said the other.

The door opened and a big lad with a butchered haircut stood there with a cigarette on the go.

'Yes?' he said, a cagefighter of a man, dressed in a shiny tight tracksuit that we could see the outline of his dick through. He had a cement jaw that could not have been broken with a sledgehammer and his right hand had lumping gold rings on all the knuckles. I imagined the damage the whole fist at full force would do to a face.

'I'm on a rickshaw,' I said. 'I have two gentlemen here looking for an after party.'

'How do you know about this place?'

'Someone told me.'

'Who is *someone?*'

'Guy called Stink.'

'Where he is?'

'I don't know.'

'Where are you from, guys?' he said to the gents.

'Cardiff,' said one.

'Well, I'm Newport originally,' said the other.

'Cardiff and Newport,' said the first. 'But both living at Cardiff now. In Cardiff. At present.'

'Welsh mens,' said the brute. 'Come in, come in. Would you like beers?'

'Yes, please.'

We walked through a kitchen and into the sitting room where a girl sat at a desk staring into a MacBook. She wore jeans hot pants and a black bikini top, a petite girl with shiny fake breasts. She was bored with it all.

Bertie was on a leather couch watching television, the remote control in one hand and a beer in the other. He nodded a hello but it looked more like a *oh, fuck you found it*. The brute spoke Russian to the girl on the MacBook. She went into the kitchen. The five of us watched her go.

'Please, take seat, watch some television,' the brute said to me. I joined Bertie over on the couch leaving the Russian to talk business with the two gents.

'Now, gentlemens, what can we do for you?'

'Just a pleasing lady,' said the first gent.

'Please,' said the other. They both looked scared. I thought they were going to run at any minute.

'Pleasing lady, this is very good,' said the Russian. 'OK, so it is three hundred pounds for one hour and if you would like additional hour or another girl afterwards we can negotiate a lower price. Credit card is no problem with discretionary billing, champagne is available, poppers, coke—whatever you want.'

The girl came back with four bottles of beer. Two for the gents. One for me, and another for Bertie. I handed mine to Bertie and he lightened up.

'So you found it, Irish?'

'I did,' I said.

'How much for only *half* an hour?' asked the first gent.

'Or even fifteen minutes?' asked the other.

'It is by hour,' said the Russian, looking to the girl as if to say, *you believe this shit?* The girl gave them a look to tell them they were a pair of tight old bastards.

'Here,' said Bertie, handing me over the remote. 'I don't know what to watch. There was some stupid film but now it's over.'

The gents counted out cash and handed it to the brute. He counted it and handed it to the girl who counted it and put it in the drawer of the desk.

'Please, gentlemens, follow me,' said the brute. The three of them left the sitting room through another door that led out into a hallway. The girl got back to her MacBook. Advertisements were on the telly. I flicked through the channels.

'Did you give them Viagra?' Bertie asked.

'Viagra?'

'You should give them Viagra. Makes them want more girl.'

I did not like the situation. The After Party angle was supposed to be a way of *avoiding* dead calms and sitting around. This seemed to be all about sitting around. I wanted to get going. My legs were gnawing at me. Trembles, shocks and shakes were beginning in them. It was out of the frying pan and into the bloody fire.

'So what?' I said to the girl on the MacBook. 'We just sit here and watch television?'

She yawned and nodded.

'Relax,' Bertie said. 'We're making money. Go now if you want. You brought two guys, one-fifty each so that makes three hundred you are on. But if your two guys go again with more girls, you won't get commission. The Russians will keep it for themselves.'

'So we wait to see if they want to have sex again after they have sex now?'

'Yes,' said Bertie, like it was obvious.

I flicked on through the channels quicker. There were late night shows with tits and guns in them. Films with tits and guns in them, too.

'Leave that one,' Bertie said but it was too late. I had flicked past and was not going back. The doorbell rang. The brute came back in from the hallway and walked straight through the room to answer it.

'Ten,' someone shouted. There was a bit of calming down, a bit of stern instruction then the Russian walked inside in the company of a young lad with a hanging jaw. He was about twenty-five, with tufts of blonde hair spiking out from his head and big red eyes full of weirdness. He started to dance around the room, pointing his fingers like guns.

'What is this? Gay place? Those are the ugliest women I've ever seen,' he said, pretend-shooting us and blowing away the pretend-smoke from the tops of his fingers. 'Got you,' he said. 'You're dead so play dead.'

Bertie played dead to humour him, grabbing his heart as though he had been shot in it. Arman walked in, closed the door behind him and sat on the matching leather armchair.

'How you been?' he said to Bertie as they shook hands. Arman seen me— 'you know about this place, Irish? Who told you?'

'Stink.'

'That rotten bastard,' said Arman, shaking his head from side to side.

'Ten. I want ten,' shouted Arman's guy. He walked over to Bertie and tried to take his glasses from off his face.

'Let me try on those glasses,' he said.

Bertie allowed it.

'Jesus Christ, man. You are blind,' he said and threw the glasses down on Bertie's lap. The young lad then noticed the girl on the MacBook.

'Now this is what I'm talking about. What's your name, baby?'

'All of the way here he's talking women, women, I want women,' Arman said.

'He says before he dies he wants to fuck ten thousand women. And I say, sure you are strong, good-looking guy—you could. And when the door open he shouts—ten, give me ten. I could not believe it. Swedish.'

'You give him Viagra?' Bertie asked.

'Two,' Arman said.

'Wow,' Bertie said, looking over at Arman's Swedish thoroughbred that was demanding ten *just like her*, pointing at the girl on the MacBook.

'You could make a million pounds with this guy,' Bertie said. 'You bastard.'

'We do not have ten girls available at the moment,' said the brute. 'How about

we start you with four?'

'Fine for now,' said the Swede. 'But I want ten after.'

'No problems,' said the brute. 'How would you like to pay?'

The Swede handed a credit card to the brute. He handed it to the girl on the MacBook who ran it.

'Can I offer you any champagne? Popper? Coke?'

'Champagne,' said the Swede and danced on over to our part of the sitting room. He jumped up on the coffee table in front of us. 'And get the little guys a bottle of champagne, too. Arman, my man, you want champagne?'

'That would be very, very nice, boss. Thank you. Very nice.'

'No problems,' said the Swede then pretend-shot him with his finger and once again blew away the pretend-smoke. The girl on the MacBook okayed the card and the brute and the Swede left the sitting room.

'That country is too dark for too much of the year,' Bertie said, swirling a finger around by the side of his head.

I flicked through the channels faster, passing car crashes and tattoo shows and music videos and documentaries on call-girls and movies ending in Mexican stand- offs and lonely girls in lingerie looking to chat right now, late night poker tournaments. I could not get right in my seat.

'Irish, pick something, you making me dizzy,' Bertie said.

The brute came back inside with a bottle of champagne in an ice bucket and three glasses. He laid it all down on the coffee table.

'Beautiful,' the brute said to Arman and shook his hand. Bertie was disgusted and made for the champagne as though it was his trophy as much as Arman's who took it from him and did the pouring. He poured himself a big glass, gave Bertie a small glass and offered me the third.

'No thanks,' I said.

'It's champagne,' Bertie said.

'I don't want any,' I said. I felt jealous that they could all have one or two drinks and it wouldn't end up in a weeklong binge of chaos and pandemonium but at the same time, I felt like I had something better with the rickshaw.

'Go on, Irish. Have some,' Arman said. He sipped from his glass. 'Mmm. So delicious and cooling and refreshing.'

'I don't want any,' I said. 'And stop with that shit.'

'Go on, Irish. It's only one glass,' he said.

'No,' I said.

'I will take it,' Bertie said, grabbing it from Arman.

The channels roared on past—televangelists and cops chasing robbers, crazy people and mental patients and shows on adjusting to having a tree for a head. More music videos and the lesson learned by the tattoo artists right before the credits and the call girl was crying because she just wanted a better life and now she was not too sure if she made the right decision and one of the Americans with sunglasses was going all-in and the commentator was getting very excited and there were more music videos and the lonely girl in lingerie was still lonely and a movie was about to start.

Upstairs, springs in a bed started to squeak. A man groaned like a bear and a headboard slammed over and over against a wall.

'He going for the big finish,' Bertie said.

The Swede *yee-haw*'ed from somewhere up there too, a cork popped, fizz spilled out and more walls heaved and the ceiling shook and lampshades swayed. There were more tits on the telly and someone was ducking out of the way of bullets. More lonely women played with phone cords on beds and an interactive roulette show host said it was *just that easy.*

And it was an appalling state of affairs I suddenly found myself in. Bringing guys to prostitutes—waiting for them while they had sex, hoping they wanted to have sex again. It was the rich buying the poor and if this was what easy money was, I didn't fucking want it.

I wanted to pedal.

To make matters worse, my phone started to ring. I took it out of my pocket. It was Niamh. I put it back in my pocket.

Arman and Bertie were looking at me.

'I can't watch this shite,' I said, getting up out of the seat. 'I've got to go.'

'You want your money now?' asked the brute, delighted with my departure.

'No,' I said, tossing the remote to Arman. 'Buy yourself a new pair of trousers. And get her a t-shirt if there's any change.'

I walked through the kitchen and out the back door. The brute followed. 'Bring back man's anytime you want. It is twenty-four hour.'

'Men,' I said. 'Man's makes it sound like you don't know the meaning of the word.'

I hopped up on my rickshaw and got going.

RUNNERS

He was Christmas-time wasted and shouted at the bouncers outside a club on Shaftesbury Avenue. 'Two hundred thousand chaps, that's what I make a year. Two hundred thousand pounds. Actually, wait one minute. Wait just one minute.' He put his finger to his lip, pretending to have had a revelation. 'I forgot to add on bonuses. How silly of me. I got a hundred thousand in Christmas bonuses. So, what's all that up to? Three hundred thousand pounds is it, chaps?'

The bouncers had heard it all before. They chewed chewing gum and shrugged their shoulders.

A group of girls approached the door.

'Know how much they make, ladies?' he asked. 'Twenty-five K a year. Know how much I make?'

One of the girls said, 'I don't care what you make. Out of the way, would ya?'

'You weren't saying that an hour ago when I was buying Dom Perignon,' he said.

'The day I let you buy me a drink is the day hell freezes over,' she said. 'Now, out of the way.'

He held the scruff of his own suit jacket tight around his neck, faked a shiver and rubbed his own arms. 'It's cold. Do you feel that? Getting cold. You bitch.'

A bouncer pushed him out of the doorway and he immediately shouted *assault* and *these people are witness.* Then he took out credit card receipts from his pocket. 'Here, nine hundred squid for champers—just like that,' he shouted inside the bar at the girls. They were long gone so he held up the receipt to the bouncers.

'Just like that,' he said again.

'Oi, you,' he called over to me. 'Rickshaw. Come here. I'll give you two hundred pounds to take me down to Barbican.'

'Whatever,' I said. Villains were fares, too and needed to get home as much as heroes.

He got on board. I looked back over my shoulder and waited for traffic to pass so that I could pull out and get going. The guy was sticking up his middle finger at the bouncers like a naughty kid on the back of a bus.

I cycled on like I had been oxygenated, freed out into a fast-flowing vein.

'What's your name then?'

'Irish,' I said, standing up off the saddle and digging deep.

'Potatoes,' he said in a Jamaican accent, trying for Irish.

I didn't mind taking shit about being Irish as long as it was funny. It was all just a laugh.

This guy though, had a mean tone disguised as all-just-a-laugh.

'You're all right,' he said. 'I'm calling you Rudolph my Irish-nose reindeer. Don't worry. I'll make this worth your while. I've got lots of money.'

Passengers who ran from the rickshaw without paying were called *runners*.

The first type of runner did not want to know anything about the rider. There was no asking of the riders' name, like country kids being warned against naming lambs and calves. If it had a name, it would be harder in the end. There was no chit-chat, no *what time are you finishing at, tonight?* or *This must keep you fit?* When the runner ran, at a traffic light or during a slow roll, the rickshaw shook hard because their adrenalin was up and they were panicked. The pedals went light and the runner would be pegging it down an alleyway or clearing a wall. This was honest running, where *runner* got its name. I probably would've been doing it myself if it was a few years earlier.

'You go down on girls, Rudolph?' he asked. 'I hear these blokes at work, and they're shouting about how they love it. Everyday I hear them. Like they're the universal understander of the pussy and their mouth is some sort of sanctuary for broken down and depressed pussy. I tell the slags straight out that I don't. They're so used to blokes doing it, you should see their faces when I tell them I don't. Looks like snow for Christmas. *Let it snow, let it snow, let it snow.*'

A loud sniff came from behind me. He changed nostril and there was another loud sniff. 'You like snow?'

'No thanks,' I said.

'All gone now anyway. Fucking wind. Just cost me a grand that wind. Whatever. And some of them are like, well if you don't go down on me I'm not going down on you. Trying to make a stand. And I'm saying to myself, yeah right you're not. And they tell their friends right in front of you that you don't do it, trying to shame you into doing it. And it's great, the friends are looking me up and down and it's got them thinking, well what am I packing? And then the girlfriends look at the boyfriends with resentment because they're not man enough like me to *not* do it.'

My legs were getting that good type of numb, I was losing breath and my heart was a pump-action shotgun, blasting delicious energy all over me, keeping me alert and alive and weightless.

'Don't get me wrong, Rudolph. If it was outlawed in the morning I'd be president of the underground resistance—just getting it arranged in secret tunnels, scurrying about in the dark just going down on it.'

The second type of runner did not run at all. This was lazy and cruel-hearted and I had little time for it. They would negotiate price, speak to the rider, ask his name and his story, have a laugh and when they got to their destination they would get out of the rickshaw and walk slowly away, that being that. The rider would get off his saddle and follow—*hey, hey money,*

you owe me money. The runner would act like they had
never seen the rider before in their life. It was awful
acting. If the rider kept walking after them down the
street wanting payment, they would choose to see it
as an attack against them, an injustice like, *what is
this guys fucking problem?* There would be a warning
from the runner, a quick break in the act, something
like—*yo, you better just forget about it, bruv.* The rider
usually did not just forget about it—he wanted his
money and *that* was that. The runner would get fero-
cious in a flash, get right up in the rider's face, maybe
even throw him a punch in the mouth, scare him
with a burst lip.

'When I'm in trouble I do it. Like, big-big, trouble. I buy her nice big diamonds and go down and
she acts like the Queen of Sheba or something. But
you know as well as I do, they can't handle the power.
Think about it right, we've oppressed them for centuries, millennia actually. Now, all of a sudden they've
equality and the right to vote and maternity leave and
they're bank managers and police-persons but rela-
tively speaking, over millennia of oppression, power
is unnatural for them. And they're bitter about it.
Ever asked them to make a decision? Like talking to a
turnip. You'd stand better chances getting a decision
from the turnip. I'm just taking a piss. I'll give you
more money for the inconvenience. You carry on.'

I looked behind to find him stood up at the side
of the rickshaw and reaching down into his trousers.
He pulled out his dick, the thing already mid-piss. It

went on his hand, his trousers and the backseat until he got the stream in control and directed it towards the road below.

'It's all just nature,' he said. 'Just nature. You talk to a prostitute, right? They know. Work sends me to Singapore sometimes. To rob the bastards blind. The usual. But Singapore right, you go to a place called *Three Floors of Whores* and the girls are behind a glass wall and you pick one out like it's a sweet shop or something, they sit there in rows smiling at you, wanting you to pick them. So you just tell hostess the one you want and away you go upstairs with her.'

He finished pissing and sat back down. The rickshaw shook, interrupting my pedalling.

'And away you go. Just upstairs with her. Easy.'

'Rich buying the poor,' I said.

'Right! Same as here. You know. Course you know for God's sake—you ride a rickshaw. No offence but this is the most visceral image of class divide there is, right? Anyway, you can take two or three of them up to the room with you if you want. I didn't. I just got the one. But you can if you want. You just have to pay more, that's all.'

Outside a pub, a group of young men dropped shot glasses full of liquor into larger glasses of energy drink and raced each other in drinking it all back. They were city lads, probably doing the 12 pubs of Christmas. The winner of the shot race, the biggest and reddest of them, championed his glass to everyone else. A young intern was in last place, gagging as he drank. The group shouted him on until he finished.

'Nice bike, fella,' one of the men said as we whizzed past.

I had not had a drop in three months. The feeling was still there, especially when I had worked up a sweat and I was thirsty. I'd remember the first taste of fizzy beer or raw vodka on my lips. I tried to remember the taste of wine sometimes. I couldn't remember if it was sour or tangy. A few days before, when I was caught up in a dead calm, I thought about taking a week off at Christmas, check into a hotel, draw myself a bath and just drink. I would have had enough money for it.

I heard my phone buzzing underneath the backseat. I pushed down on the pedals hard.

'I think your phone's ringing.'

'It's OK, just ignore it.'

Barbican was getting closer. The city was quieter, and darker. There were no more shoppers or music coming out of shop porches. There was only a fresh wind and the sound of my phone buzzing. Stopping. Then buzzing again. I did not want to answer it. Christmas time—people checking in, Niamh maybe, having visited the graves for Christmas and thinking about me, wondering how I've been, wondering where I was, wondering if I was happy. I knew it was cruel not to answer but I did not know what to say. I wanted to answer when I had an answer. When I was happy. It was why I liked London. You didn't have to be happy. You could just be anonymous.

'I caught something off of the prostitute I got, Rudolph. In Singapore. Chlamydia. I got a check done as soon as I got home. The condom broke.'

I looked behind. He was crying.

'If I told the missus it would've been over. She's always banging on about loyalty—loyalty, loyalty, loyalty. The hundred and fifty grand wedding would have been off. My parents would have to have been told. No good. Six years of a relationship wasted. The money I put into it.'

I pulled up beside Barbican tube station and stopped. My legs were aching and trembling and I used the time to catch a breath. I had the shakes in my hands.

'If I started to wear condoms she would have known something was up. She'd have had my bags packed before I knew what was what. So I've been putting antibiotics in her tea every morning,' he said, the crying becoming uncontrollable, rock-bottomed and capable of anything. 'What type of a person am I?'

My phone rang louder now that we were stopped. 'You're here. Come on, off,' I shouted.

He curled up wretched at my tone, horrified in the thing he had turned into on the back of the rickshaw. I stared at him full on, his pupils as big as two black rats.

'Is this Barbican already?'

'Yes.'

'Fast,' he said, stumbling off. He brushed himself down and straightened himself out on the footpath, wiped his eyes and coughed like nothing was up. Like nothing had happened. He took out his wallet from his inside pocket.

'Here you go,' he said, offering me his credit card. 'Take two-fifty.'

I did not take the card. His expression was wondering why. I didn't like the thought of trying to march him to an ATM to get payment. It would have kept me stopped for ten, maybe fifteen minutes. Fuck him.

The phone started to ring again. I wanted another fare as though it was oxygen, a chance to breathe again. I'd start back for Shaftesbury and surrounding streets, the lungs for lost people. If luck was on my side, I'd hopefully find someone at a bus stop trying to get back to the West End, maybe even west, down to Sloane Square or over to Hammersmith, down to Victoria even, somewhere over the other end, a good long fare.

'Oi,' he shouted. 'Don't you want money?'

The guy reminded me of when Niamh and I beat Monopoly when we were younger, amounting so much cash and hotels that the bank couldn't afford to pay us anymore, so we became the bank, exchanging large amounts of cash when we landed on each other's property. It turned into a farce, and we just laughed at its ridiculousness. Money was a sinking ship. The Murcielago's, the thousand pound bottles—banknotes would be carbon tested by archeologists in two thousand years, and we'll all be laughed at by the people of the future for our barbarism. Money was a sinking ship, Scrooge McDuck was drowning, this guy scampering up to the bow in desperation.

The phone was still buzzing. I tried to ignore it, cycling on.

I was happy Christmas was a busy time and would pass fast. Keeping busy meant I didn't have to answer the phone. Keeping busy meant I didn't have to remember. The third type of runner, I guess, was the rickshaw rider himself.

'You fucking arsehole,' the guy shouted behind me. 'I've still to pay you! Oi! I've got your fucking money you stupid Irish cunt.'

THE FALL OF ZAHIR

January was a dead calm. There was no go and money had dissolved to show its worth. People were skint, tourists scarce. Even the pickpockets were on holiday. The streets offered a skeleton crew of punters making only essential trips, eyes on their feet as they walked, resolutions and gym memberships up to the eyeballs. This irritated the cabbies and they took it out on the rickshaw riders, edging closer with their bumpers, shouting *wanker* for sport.

I was doing lifts for a pound. I didn't care.

'A pound!' people said.

'Yeah,' I said. 'A pound.'

'From here? A pound?'

'Yeah,' I said.

To Hell with money. I just wanted to stay going.

The shops were sleeping up on Oxford Street, worn out and exhausted, taking no notice of Zahir fighting a pair of runners. Fare standards had dropped and riders were giving benefit of the doubt.

'Come on, motherfuckers,' Zahir shouted. His tie and suit jacket were missing. His shirt was torn under the arms, oily and blackened at the collar. His left trouser leg was shredded from continually catching on the chainring and stuffed inside his sock. On the first day, he had been a respectable and educated young man from Bangladesh with a degree in economics, *looking to make good business for customer*, eager and bursting for a bit of work. Now, there on Oxford Street at three in the morning he was a fight-dog, poked and prod by the night streets—beeped at, roared upon, stressed out and crazed by the hard graft.

'Come on you motherfuckers. Your mothers fuck,' he shouted, charging gung-ho at the two runners to tear them both asunder. One took an easy swing and connected his fist with Zahir's mouth. Zahir held his jaw to consider a cry. It was a pitiful display.

'Zahir, come on, buddy,' I said. 'It's lost. Take it on the chin and move on.'

The runners were not rising to meet Zahir's anger. They had not been hit nor were they out of pocket but they were not backing down from the fight either, and so the pair stood and waited for Zahir to make up his mind.

'Listen to your girlfriend. You ain't getting a penny from us, bossman.'

'You thieves,' shouted Zahir and pointed them both out to Oxford Street. 'You thieving men. Thieves. These men are thieves.'

Oxford Street's shops did not care. If anything they wanted him to shut up.

'Come on, Zahir,' I said. 'Let's go.'

'You motherfuckers,' Zahir said.

The runners laughed and walked away.

Zahir pulled his hair tight at the roots with both hands and poured tears from his eyes and blood from his mouth. 'I cannot take this violence any longer, Irish,' he said. 'This hatred. This horrible people. And dishonesty. So dishonest. My third fight, Irish. I had never a fight in my life before I began this rickshaw business. I am tired. I am very exhausted, and I can no longer do this employment. So tiring. Nobody cares.'

'I care, sweetheart,' said a man who stopped at Zahir's side. He wore a tight pair of hot-pants and a yellow vest. Around his neck he wore a feathered boa. The man tilted his head in pity and looked out from his star-shaped sunglasses, puckering his lips for a kiss.

'No you do not care, sir,' said Zahir. 'You liar.'

'Don't be like that, sweetie,' said the man, tickling Zahir's face with the end of his boa.

'I am not your fucking sweetness,' shouted Zahir then ran towards his rickshaw. 'This fucking rickshaw, fuck you.' He gave the front wheel a net-busting kick. 'And this bad language that I am using. Fuck means nothing to me. It is just a word that I use to try and be heard. Fuck me, fuck this, fuck that, motherfucker and over there is fuck-all and cunt, I say cunt, Irish. Shut up you cunt, you silly bunch of cunts, you fat cunts and please stop being such a motherfucking cunt. I cannot take this type of English language. Are we in England at all? Is this Hell? I'm sorry. I'm fucking sorry.'

Zahir had flipped. There was no going back. I had seen it before.

After my mother died, my father decided that nothing made sense and life was meaningless. Work had worked on him for long enough. He quit his job of thirty years and barricaded himself inside his bedroom and when we knocked on the door, all he said was—I'm fine, just leave me alone.

Three days passed. Nothing changed. We called the doctor who arrived and asked what was the problem?

'He's locked himself inside his room, Doctor.'

'Has he mentioned that it's all not worth living?'

'No, just to leave him alone. That he's fine.'

The doctor climbed to the top of the stairs.

'I'm fine. Just leave me alone,' my father shouted before the doctor had a chance to even knock.

The doctor came back down the stairs and asked that he be called if anything changed. Then he left. We sat in the kitchen, drank tea and waited for everything to go back to normal.

Another day passed.

We phoned the priest, a young Polish lad just out of the seminary. He arrived and climbed to the top of the stairs, knocked on the door and announced himself. My father burst-opened the door, grabbed the young priest by the collar and threw him against the wall.

'Never step foot in this house again,' my father said then looked down to us from the landing. 'I'm sorry. I'm very sorry,' he said. 'I just can't do it anymore.'

'I can't do it anymore, Irish,' Zahir said. He sat down on the edge of the footpath and the street went on without him. He was gone.

'I'll bring your rickshaw back to Vasily if you want?'

'Thank you, Irish.'

'Take care, Zahir.'

'Take care, Irish.'

We shook hands, his shake like a vice.

I rested the front wheel of Zahir's rickshaw on my backseat so that it was towable, gave Zahir a goodbye salute and pedalled back to the base where Vasily was thrashing the place in search of his ferret. He had bought it to catch the mice, which were becoming a serious problem at the base. He had championed the animal about when he first bought it like it was the annihilator of vermin, the reckoning for all mice.

'His name, Maximus,' Vasilly had shouted while holding the ferret up over his head and under a spotlight. The ferret just looked uncomfortable.

It was a week later and the mice still had full run of the joint. The ferret hadn't been seen in three days. I thought Stink might have stolen it.

Vasily stopped the search and looked at the rickshaw I was carrying.

'Zahir,' I told him. 'He won't be coming back.'

'He had accident?'

'No,' I said. 'He flipped.'

'What is this flipped?'

'Like, he went a bit crazy.'

Vasilly took a look at Zahir's rickshaw to make sure it was in working order and that there really had been no accident, checking the wheels, and the differential then lifted it off my backseat and checked the steering.

'What he say?'

'Just that he couldn't do it anymore.'

'This Zahir guy never laughed. If you don't laugh, you will flip.'

'It's only when we are lost that we can truly find ourselves.'

'You think Maximus is doing this? This fucking ferret is finding himself?'

'Maybe,' I said and cycled on.

IMRUS

Imrus was from a country that no longer existed, seventy years old if he was a day. Some said sixty, others eighty. He was hyper-wrinkled and unsymmetrical, staring the world down with one eye, leaving the other away in reserve. He had been a millionaire from the rag trade down in the East End before his brain warbled. That's what Martha had said. I had asked her what the rag trade was and she ignored the question. Imrus's wife had left him, sold the house out from under him, cleaned out the accounts, took the mattress-stash then fled to an unknown tropical location leaving poor old brain-warbled Imrus with enough for a deposit and the first two week's rent on a rickshaw. It was simply amazing he could do the work at his age. Whatever it may have been.

'Imrus is a madman,' Martha had said. 'Therefore, Imrus has the strength of a madman.'

Imrus was around the West End twenty-four hours a day. That's why we began to know of each other. Often we were the only two rickshaws about, monitoring each other's movement from afar in case one knew something the other did not.

At night in the base, when I would be about to fall asleep on my backseat, I would see Imrus arriving back. He was always the last rider to pack it in, and would only ever do so when the streets were silent. He would pour himself a cup of tea from his flask then crawl into the fire hose cupboard.

'That's one thing I would never do is be homeless like you and Imrus,' Bertie said one day. 'I need my own roof, you know? That's why I'm all the time building tree houses. Just in case. Where do you two even wash?'

'The bathroom sink,' I said.

'You are animals,' Bertie said, looking around to make sure there were no eavesdroppers. 'I think Imrus ate Vasilly's ferret. Don't tell him I said this.'

One lunchtime, Imrus braked beside me in Holborn outside the supermarket. The office workers were walking around us with their burritos, prawn wraps and midday cappuccinos.

'I have been meaning to tell you, Irish, those clothes you have are filthy. Next time you are in Camden, buy some new ones in the market. The guys will bring them to you so you will not need to leave your rickshaw.'

'OK,' I said.

'Could you please watch my rickshaw, Irish? I want to go inside and buy a sandwich.'

'No problem, Imrus.'

He slid off the saddle and stood at a right angle to himself, an inverted *L* with giant kangaroo thighs and little T-rex arms. He looked up at me, a sweat-matted piece of comb-over dangling down the side of his face.

'You sure you are going to watch over it?'

'Yes. Sure.'

'Ok, I am going in here,' he said and gave the street a look-over, up, down. Up

again. 'Ok, this now. I am going inside.'

'I'll watch your rickshaw for you.'

'I watch you, Irish. You work hard. I trust people who work hard. My wife, she never work one day in her whole life. Stole all my money. You can watch my rickshaw, yes?'

'I'll watch it.'

'You are starting to give lifts for a pound, Irish?'

'No,' I said. If word got out I was doing lifts for a pound, riders would have got up in arms as it damaged the market. Riders took it that seriously.

'It's OK,' Imrus said, 'I give lifts for free sometimes. It's better than sitting around, yes?'

'It might be,' I said.

He walked inside the supermarket. I could see him through the windows. He scouted the area around the sandwich fridge like he was casing the joint, looked around over his shoulder casually but not casual at all. A security bloke walked closer and Imrus started to argue with him until asked to leave.

He was like my father after *he* had warbled. Everywhere my father had gone there was drama, like he was a square peg constantly trying to squeeze himself into a universe of round holes. There was something off in the way he held himself, something slightly askew after he had rejected existence. He had been sneering, and hostile, and the people who had to live in everyday existence sensed it from him, and were constantly asking him to leave places, too. I guess he had taken to whiskey because it eased the transition.

'Please, Irish,' Imrus said on coming outside, still being watched by security. 'Can you watch my rickshaw at the next supermarket? This one is no good.'

We cycled to the next one.

My father had sat up at bars drinking whiskey until he felt the time was right for a scene, phoning the Gardaí who had arrested him the night before, calling them all sons of bitches, telling them exactly where they could find him if they had a problem with being called a son of a bitch. He had thrown glasses and put chairs through windows, crashed cars and tried to take on the world.

At the next supermarket, Imrus picked two sandwiches then raced with them to the checkout, paid for only one and left the other with the attendant. He came outside and inspected the packaging on the sandwich for tampering.

'You got one.'

'Yes,' he said. 'They may have been messing with it. I have to check.'

He opened up the sandwich and sniffed it.

'Check for what?'

'Poison. My wife's family is trying to poison me, Irish. They think I murder her so they are trying to get revenge on me.'

'How would they know what exact sandwich you would pick?'

'It's her family, Irish,' he said, 'they poison all the sandwiches. Every sandwich. They don't care. They are bloodthirsty for revenge. They try to puncture me all the time. They are trying to kill me.' Imrus looked around the street at the crowd of faces and something all of a sudden struck him as suspect. He binned the sandwich and hopped up on his rickshaw. 'They cannot catch me on this though. They cannot follow me on the rickshaw. The traffic you see, Irish. I can dip in and out. They cannot. They most certainly cannot.'

And then he cycled on.

QANNIQ

'Go on boy,' shouted an Irish lad in a leprechaun hat. 'Ride it like you stole it.'

It was St. Patrick's Day.

My mother had always hated it. My father, Niamh and I would go off gallivanting in the early afternoon, drink ourselves stupid and she would have to deal with the three separate fall-outs that came stumbling in the back door at all hours—crying, bleeding, raging, senseless.

'Drank yourselves stupid,' she'd say the next day.

'Relax,' we'd say, sick as parrots.

'Nonsense of a day,' she'd say.

'Yeah right, Mam,' we'd say, like she didn't have a clue how it was. 'It's celebrating St. Patrick. He's like, our patron saint.'

'Is that right? I didn't see you at Mass celebrating your patron saint.'

'Had a tequila for him,' we'd say and giggle.

It was three in the afternoon and the queue for the Irish pub in Chinatown went down the street and around the corner. The queue wore Roscommon,

Waterford, Dublin and Carlow county colours, Irish rugby tops, Leinster and Munster jerseys, tricolours draped across its back. The lads hurried their cans of lager on reaching the front of the queue while the girls all drank what they could of their chardonnay then gave the remainder to waiting winos.

The bouncers let fifteen more punters in every five minutes. Frayed-looking bar staff took thirty-second cigarette breaks in between changing a keg then ran back inside to throw out pints. When a door opened, I saw the crowd inside, squashed in against one another, no place to even rest a drink, heads slogging ale and porter, charging hard to the bar for more, waving notes for attention. And I thought, for a moment, I saw my father in there, drinking the bar dry, happy in the state of himself, staggering, falling, bringing down whole tables of drinks as he went.

'You can't move in there,' one couple said when they came out.

I brought them home, up to Angel, no charge.

Scotland had played Brazil in a friendly up at the Emirates Stadium and the Scots piled into the West End after the match in droves, drinking to their defeat alongside the Irish. Three Scots flagged me down on Shaftesbury Avenue and threw into the backseat, a fourth, horizontal Scotsman, nude from the waist down.

'Take Alastair here on, he's cooked,' one said, offering me a Scottish twenty and the hotel room key card. I took the key but not the twenty.

'It's free,' I said.

'He's getting payment some other way,' another said and the three Scots had a laugh.

'He likes to be told how pretty he is,' they shouted.

'Cunts,' Alastair mumbled.

I cycled on, through traffic, weaving around the buses on New Oxford Street until I was eventually stopped at a red light. Arman pulled up close to my side with a load of Irish singing the *Wild Rover* in his backseat.

Arman did not say a word. He stared straight ahead and watched the lights. He had been different since Zahir left, as though it had been my fault because I hadn't persuaded Zahir otherwise, probably seeing it as me doing my best to take competition off the streets.

I got Alastair to the Travel Lodge up on Kings Cross Road. 'You're here.'

'Where?' he said with slobber hung down his chin and front.

'At your hotel.'

'Who are you?'

'I brought you here. You're on a rickshaw.'

'What the fuck?' said Alastair, looking around and indeed, found himself on the back of a rickshaw. He knew something else was the matter but he was not quite sure what yet. He opened his arms and legs out in spread-eagle position to inspect himself.

'Where's my kilt?'

'You didn't have it on when they threw you on.' He made certain I was not wearing it.

'I'd nine hundred pound in me sporran.'

'Your friends probably have it.'

'Aye an' all,' he said, and stepped off. I handed him his key card. He did not ask how I had it. He staggered bare-arsed into the hotel's lobby. The receptionist looked up from her computer screen.

'I really fancy you,' shouted Alastair. 'So how about it, eh?'

The receptionist looked back to her screen. It was nothing she hadn't seen before.

I cycled on.

When I got back into Soho, doorways had filled up with dipped heads of Colins, Ewans and Jims. There was going to be lots more lifts. I was happy.

The Irish noticed the Scottish in the doorways across the street. 'All too much for you Scottish boys is it?'

The Colins, Ewans, and Jims sorted themselves out, stood up straight, not to be out-drunk by their cousins from across the water. A leprechaun went running down Old Compton with a policeman's hat. Two hatted cops and one hatless cop went tearing after him.

'You boys not have hats in Ireland?' shouted the Scottish.

'At least we have trousers,' shouted the Irish.

'They don't make troosers big enough for our massive horse dicks,' shouted the Scottish.

'The only thing you boys have in common with horses is that most of yis are on ketamine,' shouted the Irish.

'And the rest of us are on yer mothers,' shouted the Scottish and stuck out their chests. The Irish did the same.

A group of Hare Krishna's came skipping around the corner in their sandals and robes with banners and drums, tapping on finger-cymbals, knees getting thrown as high as possible into the air, their pony-tails getting flung about, all of them chanting, *Hare Krshna, Hare Krshna, Hare Krshna, Hare Krshna.*

'Mental bunch of cunts,' said the Irish and the Scottish together. They all started laughing and crossed the street to shake hands and then they all made for the pub, arguing about distillation but agreeing that Donegal was beautiful.

Niamh had come back from Australia with it all sorted out. Whatever demons she had had, she was settled with them. She had got engaged over there when she had found out there was a baby on the way. She was partied-out anyway, she had said. When I asked her how it was, she had said it was just like Ireland but in a different place.

The Irish pub was closing. The Irish and the Scottish inside drank back what was left then begged the bar staff for just one more. The bar staff flat-out refused. The music was switched off. The bouncers put some pressure on with extra loud shouts and the crowds flushed; Galway jerseys and Celtic tops, Siobhans, Jims, Alastairs, Seans, Colins, and John-Pauls, Connaught rugby jerseys, red beards, green wigs, bagpipes, sporrans and bodhrans. It was a mob.

Blind. Destroyed. Fried. Loaded. Obliterated. Pie-eyed. Shit-faced. Zonked. Toasted. Pickled. Stewed. Out onto the street to a cold wind and waiting rick-shaws. Their eyes looked like they all wanted some-thing more. They wanted the whole thing to keep going. They were all plastered. Gee-eyed. Twisted. Mangled. Langered. Locked. Mouldy. Ossified.

A leprechaun in a police hat was walking around with his shoulders full of authority, telling everyone they were nicked.

The cab drivers were taking none of them home—no way.

The cops didn't know what to do, stretched, sad and out of wind, like they were realising no matter what they did there would still be shit. Over and over and over. A chopper flew about in the sky radioing down to the guys on the ground about this incident and that incident but they could not arrest half that deserved it, or call an ambulance for even half that looked like they may need one. Instead they arrested a few of the worst, the very angry men that booze had taken to that bad place, who knew there was some meaning in it somewhere, who weren't getting what they wanted to do done, who knew the ridiculousness of something but could not quite grasp it, who felt they had been promised something but booze had reneged on that promise, and had punched walls or men to express it.

When I was twelve, I bought a catapult at a county show. It was called *The Black Widow*. It was the coolest thing I had ever seen in my life. I wanted to destroy something with it. I sneaked it home in my jumper and slept with it under my pillow. The next day I used it to break every window on my Uncle Henry's tractor. It was an old tractor. I thought he didn't use it anymore. I thought everybody would be fine with it. They were not. My punishment was to work with Uncle Henry on his farm for the Easter holidays. He gave me the worst jobs imaginable—emptying gutters, sweeping sheds, pulling yellow weeds out of his beet. After a few days of it, when he seen he had broken me, he eased up and we drove around checking on his sheep. They would stick their heads through the square wire fencing to get at grass in the next field and we would have to pull them out.

'Why are they doing this?' I asked. 'They've got lots of grass in the field they're in.'

'People always want more don't they? Same with sheep,' Henry said, and that was that.

The cops had closed all of the 24-hour beer and wine shops around the West End and waited for the mob to burn itself out.

'Lightweight,' lads called other lads who were drunker than themselves, like it was a boxing match, an endurance test, a fight to either win or lose.

Two Irish lads were pushing, threatening and warning one another, the warm- up for a good old punch-up outside the pub.

'I didn't go near her, Roy—right,' said the bigger of the two. The mere mention of *her* enraged little

Roy and he reached for the throat, catching hold of the scruff then delivered him a punch across the chin. The punch was nothing serious but more than the big lad could calmly handle. He swept Roy's feet out from under him, pinning him to the ground.

Martha rolled to my side and nodded. We watched the fight together.

Roy played dead. The big lad let him up. Roy stood for a moment then something flash-boiled inside him and he launched himself towards the pharmacy's window beside the pub, landing it with a head-butt while both his feet were still off the ground. The window cracked out in a big snowflake and the burglar alarm screamed out across the street. Roy was not finished. He started to bash the window with his fist.

'Fucking bitch,' he shouted.

He got hold of himself and walked away without another word.

Some years back, the Ballybailte's bank manager came to a settlement with Henry for one hundred thousand euros on a two hundred thousand euro debt. Henry then sold his farm when it was rezoned as residential. The bank manager heard of the sale and came looking for the rest of the money. Henry reminded him of the settlement. The bank manager was not having it and sent him a solicitor's letter. Henry drank a half a bottle of whiskey, took his shotgun down to the bank, shot out its windows and then sat down to wait for the sergeant who eventually arrived and arrested him. He took Henry back to the station, helped him with the remainder of the whiskey and played cards with him all night. In the morning he was released and told to sort himself out.

'A mad man's drink,' my Aunt called whiskey.

'Is madness beneath us all just waiting to burst out?' I asked.

'If madness is beneath us,' she said, 'this town is the fucking Saudi Arabia of madness I can tell you that.'

The bank did not pursue for the money, nor did they prosecute, or even send a bill for replacing its windows. Henry was elected to a seat in Dail Eireann a year later.

'Guys are flootered tonight,' I said to Martha.

'Flootered?'

'Drunk,' I said. 'Like the Eskimos with forty words for snow.'

'Qanniq,' Martha said.

'What?'

'The Inuit language adds prefixes and suffixes to a stem word. It may seem like they have many words for snow but they only have one. It's qanniq.'

The big lad picked up Roy's phone that had fallen out of his pocket in the tussle. 'You forgot your phone you crazy bastard,' he said and flung it at Roy who was walking towards me. The phone caught Roy square-on in the back of the head and exploded into ten different pieces; SIM card, buttons, battery and covers going all over the place. Roy did not seem to care about having his own phone smashed off the back of his head and kept walking.

'Actually, you know what, Roy?' the big lad shouted. 'I *did* fuck her. She was a little humdinger so she was.'

Roy sprinted back at him for round two.

'The romantic notion,' Martha continued, 'is that the Inuits see snow differently because of the forty different words they have to describe it.'

FULL MOON

Occasionally, a bike locked to a rack would drop to the ground. Maybe a wheel would be on the street in danger of being driven over. The people who picked them up and put them straight again were always bike-owners themselves.

'I own a bike myself,' they would say. 'So I know.'

The Chinese girl looked like a dropped bike. She was new but bruised, through the wars already, dressed in a short skirt and knee-high boots. Her coat was white plastic. Her boyfriend's hands were locked on her windpipe and tightening. She tried to pry them off but stood no chance, the boyfriend built like a Panzer, a mean bastard with purpled scars on his face from knife fights. He ran a walk-up on Dean Street. If business was slow, he marched his girlfriends around Soho and pointed out lone men for them to approach and propose a blowjob to, up Dansey Place, a dark alleyway in the middle of Chinatown. After fifteen minutes the girlfriend would return, hand over the cash and he would hand back a small amount of cocaine wrapped in cling film. She would snort it in one then wait for him to point out another lone man.

The Chinese girl took her hands away from her boyfriend's hold and allowed the strangle. Her eyes met mine and said, *I'm fine. Just leave me alone.*

I couldn't stand for it.

My plastic tyre-pump smashed off the guy's head and broke in half. *You're on your own, Irish, you idiot,* it said.

'Run,' I said to Chinese girl who had not moved, who had caught taste of death and nothingness and now wanted the whole plate.

'Where?' she said and I knew I was rightly screwed.

'Get on the back,' I said, nodding my head towards the rickshaw.

'You is dead man,' the guy said and advanced, intent on pulverising me. I backed away and he chased me around the rickshaw. He stopped. I stopped, the rickshaw between us. He faked a left then went right. I didn't take the bait and went right, too, the rickshaw still ending up between us. And on like this I thought it would go forever, around and around.

'It was an accident,' I said.

'My fists are going to have accident,' he said, interrupted by the butt of a wine bottle clonking him on the head. Down he went, the little Chinese girl standing over him, about to bring the wine bottle down on his face until I caught her arm and pushed her up on the rickshaw.

I hopped up on the saddle, baddie defeated and fair maiden on board, tearing off up Shaftesbury Avenue, twenty-five thousand miles in front of us before we got back to where we were.

'You are stupid,' the Chinese girl said. 'You are very stupid.'

I cycled up through Covent Garden, wanting a downhill so that I could think for a minute. I took Bow Street, passed the Royal Opera House, the crowds all coming out after a lovely evening of *La Bohème*. There was a small cycle path through to the Waterloo Bridge intersection. I took it just before the light turned red.

The Chinese girl reached forwards from the backseat and head-locked me with her arms.

Everything went black. I reached for her arms instead of the brakes, losing control of the steering. I felt us veer off-left but I couldn't find the handlebars in the dark to amend and then came the beeping horns, rickshaw eating up road at high speed, the city out there somewhere, a crazy Chinese girl laughing hysterically.

We hit footpath and slammed to a stop, my groin taking another pounding on the front steering column. Children were becoming less and less likely in my future as the rickshaw days went on. I pulled her hands away and there the city was once more, cars, buses and black cabs stopped all around, us in the middle, a full moon high up in the sky.

'Are you fucking crazy?' yelled a cabbie.

'Yes,' shouted the Chinese girl. 'I am the crazy fucking girl with the bulimia and the running-away-from-home, OK? Yes, I am the crazy. Suck your dick, baby? You want me to suck your dick?'

The outmatched cabbie rolled up his window and drove on down Aldwych without another word. Traffic manoeuvred around us in the middle of the intersection. The Chinese girl sat back in the back-seat. 'Poor baby,' she said. 'Did you hurt your little, stupid balls?'

'You're a crazy,' I said. 'Get the fuck off my rickshaw.'

'The bridge,' she said and smacked me across the head. 'Take the bridge.'

I cycled on towards the bridge. The Chinese girl changed tune. She hugged me from behind and started to kiss at my neck. 'What you got for this job?' she whispered. 'Speed? I make your balls better if you give me some.' She slid her hands down my shorts, the world's first rickshaw reach-around.

'I don't have any drugs.'

'You are useless and stupid,' she said and sat back.

'I should take you somewhere—home or something.'

'You are going to take me back to China?'

'I'll take you to a train station, maybe? Pick a place off the departures board and go there, start again.'

'Stop,' she shouted and I obeyed. She took off her knee-high boots and threw them at oncoming traffic.

'Don't do that,' I said.

'Fuck you,' she said and jumped off the backseat, quickly climbing up on the parapet of the bridge.

'What are you doing?' I said, getting off and moving towards her.

'Stop,' she said. 'Do not come here.' She rested her bare shins against the protective bar and leaned over the Thames. 'Do you think I could fly?'

'No,' I said. People had stopped to look, asking each other what was going on, getting their phones out. 'Please come down. I think there's people over there calling the cops.'

She laughed like cops were no big deal.

'Do you think I will be mermaid if I jump?'

'No you won't end up a mermaid. Get down to fuck.'

'I think a mermaid would be nice. You could swim and swim and everything will be beautiful.'

'Come on, I can take you home. Or to a train station. Wherever you want to go.'

'You cannot take me where I want to go,' she said, leaning further forwards, lifting her arms at right angles to her body. If I moved to her she would jump. I could feel it. And London went on around us, and would go on, generations going around and around, making the same mistakes and the wheels kept on spinning and the Chinese girl was about to throw herself off the bridge.

I thought of the alcoholism pamphlets I used to recite to my Dad in vain attempt to stop him drinking—Krebs cycles and mitochondria and sensible words for chaotic situations, words that just never translated properly from page to life.

'What's she doing?' asked a woman to my side. 'Get down off there.'

'My Dad threatened to kill himself,' I said to the Chinese girl. 'All the time before he died. He was sick, you know? Depressed maybe. So, I know what you're thinking. People have problems. But, please, please come down. Things will get better.'

The Chinese girl turned around and looked at me.

'Good,' I said, reaching out to help her down.

She closed her eyes then back-flipped into the open space behind, dropped and was gone.

The onlookers screamed from the fright.

I ran to the parapet and looked over to see her hit the bow of a moored boat down there, break her back and slide lifeless into the water. Down by the bank, people raced for life buoys but she was dead and sinking. Heroes dived in to the freezing water. Twenty people called emergency at once. Sirens were already on their way.

In the pamphlets, there were the three C's for family members of the alcoholic to always remember. They needed counselling as much as the alcoholic as it turned out. *You didn't Cause it, You can't Control it and you can't Cure it.* It was what I found myself saying over and over as I pedalled away. The woman shouted at me to stop, that I needed to stay exactly where I was and give the police a statement.

You didn't cause it.

I forced my thighs to burn and mortify.

You can't control it.

I held strength clenched in my arms.

You can't cure it.

I kicked into full speed and got going.

The bike thieves sprouted up like mushrooms in shit, scouting the racks for lock-loose wheels and flimsy cable locks, bolt-cutter boners in their track-suit pants.

The butter-wouldn't-melt guys, the not-doing-nothing-to-no-one-officer guys, whispered *blow* about, *need blow?*

The phone snatchers waited by the tube exits.

The human signs pointed the crowd in a direction of late opening bars that charged exorbitant admissions.

The traffic wardens filled their quotas.

The Tellytubbies with the breast cancer buckets counted through the coin to see how much they'd scored then complained about the new Tellytubbies walking around saturating the Tellytubby market.

The long-lost friends arrived and put their arms around the drunk's shoulders and snatched their wallets with their free hand.

The couples on first dates kissed goodbye, the girl hailed a black cab and zipped off home with a smile on her face then the guy jumped on his phone for the old reliable.

Arman said, 'What's wrong guys? Want a hug?'

Stink waited at the doors of the walk-ups and asked the punters just where the hell they thought they were going.

'Upstairs,' said the punters.

'You pay first,' Stink said and the punters handed over sixty pounds. Stink hightailed it once the punters walked up the stairs and one minute later the punters came running back down the stairs shouting, *bastard, bastard, bastard.*

I stopped pedalling up outside Fahim's Kebabs on Old Compton Street and the night slung on past like a dead animal. Fahim's heaved with piss-heads. Kebab foils were thrown across the street faster than the road-sweeping machines could pick them up.

The man in the dress showed up. He turned down Moor Street and then backtracked. 'I don't believe this,' he said, as he always said, on loop, a man walking around the West End every night of the week, not believing the situation happening to him. The kebab-mongers with slop on their chins asked him if he was all right.

'All in the limo havin' a laugh,' said the man in the dress. 'And they throw this—this dress on me. So I says, fair enough—it's me stag do and that. All part of it to look a tit. Next thing, the limo stops and they throw me out—no money, no phone—nothing. And I don't know how to get back to the hotel. So I'm stranded.'

The crowd, as always, made a collection for him to get back to his hotel. He was fiend, a liar, preying on the drunk. I had had enough of the man in the dress. I cycled towards him.

'I'll give you a lift back to your hotel,' I said loudly so that the kebab-mongers heard.

'I wouldn't have enough for a rickshaw,' said the man in the dress.

'A pound,' I said. 'I'll do it for a pound.'

'Well, there you go,' said the leading kebab-monger, handing me a pound. 'Take the poor man back to his hotel.'

The man in the dress lumbered aboard the rickshaw with reluctance and waved goodbye and thanks to the kebab-mongers.

'What're you playin' at?' he said, having dropped the lost and helpless act. 'Just let me off around the corner. Oi! Let me off.'

'I'm bringing you home,' I said. 'South Kensington wasn't it?'

I broke a red light on Piccadilly Circus.

'This is ridiculous,' said the man in the dress.

I looked over my shoulder. He was calculating a jump. I pedalled faster to stop him.

I thought—if the road ahead was the future and the moment we were in is now, then as soon as *now* happens, it becomes the past—that was fast, faster than a pedal, faster than even the thought of a pedal. I thought, if *now* could somehow be grabbed hold of then it could be possible to ride with it into the past, like grabbing hold of a passing mermaid. I pedalled harder, upping the tempo. If it worked, I thought,

I've invented time travel. There was a moment of exhilaration until a bus roared past. My pupils reflected big and black in its wax-smudged windows. The time travel concept became like sticky-hot cling film on my brain and no longer made as much sense. I tried head-butting the bus windows, a whisker away from connecting, warning it not to come any closer.

The normal people inside watched me until the bus roared on. Black gas wisped up at me from its exhaust. I gulped the fumes in deep and laughed aloud, not to give the bus the satisfaction.

My knee twinged.

I pedalled on against it, biting down on my t-shirt to manage the pain, bit it through and my incisors grated off one another. Then came another twinge, a sorer one that was not going away. I wanted a sledge-hammer to whack the knee a series of tremendous blows until it fell back into line.

And right then, there was a moment of breath, a slight piece of everything being fine, a tiny fleeting moment of purpose and reason.

'Stop,' said the man in the dress and I remembered he was in the backseat, not really going home at all.

'You're a liar,' I shouted. 'There's real stranded people out there.'

'Let me off,' he shouted.

I pedalled on, half man, half bicycle, rocketing towards Hyde Park Corner and smashed another red light. Tyres screeched. The horns came horrendous and loud. The traffic readjusted itself for me and I felt all-powerful, like the drunks who stopped traffic with an outstretched hand while crossing Charing Cross Road.

'I'm nothing like you,' I shouted.

'Please stop,' said the man in the dress and I felt sorry for him. He truly was stranded now—not pretending anymore.

'I'm sorry,' I said. 'I can take you home—to where you really live, no charge.'

'Stop or I'll tip it,' he said, taking hold of both sides, ready to rock the rickshaw, a capsizing being a safer option to him than carrying on. I banked left across Grosevnor and stopped. He jumped off, landing on his knees, his dress rising over his waist, his white arse getting lit up by the headlights coming up from Victoria.

I stood up on my crossbar, undid my belt and took a piss.

'You're an animal,' the man in the dress screamed. 'An animal.'

I watched the bright yellow droplets full of empty taurine cartridges and spent caffeine shells splatter off the front wheel. I played with the stream—it was a beautiful arc to the ground that ended in a big fat splash.

'And you stink,' he screamed.

The full moon cut a sharp circle in the sky like a brake disc burnt molten. Maybe I preyed on the stranded, too. Maybe I was just like the man in the dress. Maybe I was a fiend, too. A predator.

I tucked myself back in. The man in the dress was gone and the piss trickled down the gutter. I cycled on before my muscles had time to seize, howling up to the brake disc, using her pull to re-enter my world at Marble Arch, turning onto Oxford Street, racing past the lady who put a cardboard box over her head. It was the same old box all the time, tattered and stinking. She carried it around the West End and Oxford Street, sitting down at the bus stops and putting it over her head when it all got too rough. Inside, she talked things over with herself, calmed herself down and spoke to him, whoever he was, reliving when he left, what she could have said to stop him, how she could have said it, telling him what she's doing these days and how she's coping, keeping him up to speed with what she was thinking, getting angry with him, forgiving him.

I passed the rageaholics kicking bins, the monstered men, the lunatics and the moon-juiced, the shouting drunks and the drug-crazed who were finally afraid of nobody, pot-valiant and chemically enhanced, getting up in people's faces, stomping through pedestrianized zones with fists clenched.

I howled down to the jumpers on the train platforms below, steadying themselves before the leap onto the tracks before they became just another *person under the train* announcement, and I screamed down to the swelling black Thames full of swimming mermaids, and down through the tectonic plates, through the magma and back up into the psychiatric wards where the restraints returned a rattle in solidarity.

My knee felt like it had a hot knife twisting underneath the bone. I stopped and held it beside the ghost bike at the bottom of Tottenham Court Road. It was a bike that had been spray-painted completely white and locked to a traffic light. It remembered a mowed down cyclist, going about their life one minute, a bang and a flash later they were brown bread. Before the Chinese girl killed herself on Waterloo Bridge, I would ask myself, why had they chosen to freeze the way someone died in time? Why had they made their death what we remember?

'My blood is in your veins,' my father had said on the night he died. 'My blood is in your veins, boy.'

I needed a fare.

Restarting

I needed a fare.

I wished for the worlds stranded on my backseat—whole populations of lost needing home. I wished I had great, big continents of people aboard.

Marathon day was a good start.

A Kenyan had already set a new London record, given the BBC an interview and was back at his hotel unwinding. 30,000 others were in a running river of steam, huffing and wheezing their way towards the finish, fainting, cramping and spasming, keeling over and fighting on inside terrified and trembling bodies. They ground out cartilage in their knees, irrevocably damaged shins and lower backs, pounded away at ankles and golf-ball blisters, finishing up at St. James's Park where they iced their swelling, massaged away pain, and cried. Others were wrapped in foil, shaking back and forth, staring into space like nutters. Worn-out guys used the last ounce of strength to get down on one knee, saying to their girlfriends that the last year has been the happiest time of their life, the girlfriends saying—*yes, of course, yes.*

I needed a fare.

The first was always the hardest. It tore away repairs that had been attempted by the body during the night. He was a marathon runner to Mayfair, snivelling and holding his ribcage, having ran to raise funds for a drug rehabilitation charity—'Bad I was, Irish. I showed up to a meeting once completely wired, punched out half the lads there, got thrown out, told them I was going to shoot their families, got chased by police and paid into a cinema where I called my sister and my two ex-fiance's to come get me. They all found me passed out in Alvin and the Chipmunks. Just here, Irish, thanks.'

I restarted.

Another marathon runner, a woman who cried all the way up to Euston. I asked her if she was OK—'Never better, love, never better,' she said.

I was getting that good type of numb.

My head was clearer.

I could think.

I restarted down at the Leicester Square ticket booths, looking for the hurried who fumbled around with maps that had their theatre circled with biro and had been told that curtain-up was in half an hour.

'Where's Lion King, mate?'

I restarted.

The post theatre crowds were more intense, more concentrated, the curtain-downs happening within a half hour of each other all across the West End. A route had to be calculated depending on the weather, the day, the season and the price of the show—one not doing too well will cut rates, offer web-deals, attracting those on budgets—the thrifty; the walkers, who didn't even trust lifts I told them were absolutely free.

'A pound?' one man said. 'To Russell Square, from here?'

'Yeah,' I said, 'a pound.'

The weather was heating up.

April passed and May began.

The London Cab Authority had paid for a slandering campaign. They smeared their scientific experiment the rickshaw crash on the LCD screens around the streets. The dummy got decapitated on loop.

The bad publicity in the newspapers returned as a result, reminding the public of a 170-year-old law originally designed to punish horse-cart drivers and recommended it be dusted off and put into practice— *A rogue rickshaw rider could then be arrested instantly for dangerous behaviour and his rickshaw confiscated* wrote the *Evening Standard.* Under the 170-year-old law, resting on a double yellow line would be considered a dangerous act to public safety. To top it off, they put rickshaw riders in the same final sentence as rapists, drug dealers and knife carriers, and suggested the West End needed to be cleaned of the lot.

Vasily summoned me through Arman. I hoped he wanted me to write another letter to the Evening Standard in exchange for more time to pay the rent I owed. I picked a quiet time and made for the base to avoid being chased down and making it worse.

There was a collage of fines glued on the wall of Vasily's enclosure, made out to Milli Vanilli, Mahatma Gandhi and Kurt Cobain, at addresses like Buckingham Place and 14 Bighouse, England Road, London. I had noticed community officers handing out £35 fines as fast as they could write the things—for resting on the double yellow, resting on wavy lines, resting on footpaths. It was a joke and everyone had treated it as much, even the community officers.

Vasily was on edge more than usual. His phone did not stop ringing. I took the time to charge *my* phone, it having been dead for weeks. *26 Missed Calls, 15 messages* and *12 Voicemails* when it came to life. All Niamh.

Vasily's calls were coming from the storerooms of supermarkets and the back of fast food restaurants, guys wanting out or international students arriving four months early for university and trying to make tuition fees. Everyone wanted tourist money now that it was the season, having heard Chinese whispers of Saudi Arabian princes giving two thousand pound tips all winter.

'I have no more fucking rickshaw,' Vasily shouted down the phone as soon as he answered, hanging up without waiting for a response. The phone started to ring again four seconds later. He ignored it.

'Where is Stink, Irish?'

'Haven't seen him.'

'You is friends.'

'I wouldn't call it friends.'

'Where he is?'

'I don't know.'

'You tell him he is dead. He messed with Yuri business.'

Vasily had still not found Maximus the ferret but his BLT's were being mysteriously devoured. 'This fucking bullshit ferret. I buy him to catch mice and he sneak around eating my fucking sandwich. You know Yuri?'

'No,' I said.

'He is missing a Chinese girl.'

'I don't know any Chinese girls.'

'He said guy on rickshaw took her. Describe him like you.'

'I don't know anything about it.'

'You telling me bullshit?'

'No.'

'Rent is eighty-five now. Summer—more tourists. More tourists—more money. More money—more rent. And you still owe me three weeks plus this week.'

I didn't care but I just didn't have it. 'I'll get it,' I said. 'No problem. Do you want me to write a letter for you?'

'No more letters. We is finding journalist to break his fingers.'

Arman arrived with a smiling companion in a chestnut suit, completely ignoring my presence.

'Boss, this is Zahir. He is very good rickshaw rider for you.'

The new Zahir stood there, smaller than the old Zahir but every bit as eager, looking respectful and employable and bursting for a bit of work. He thought I was of importance and shook my hand, the shake soft and barely there. Arman broke up the shake and pointed the new Zahir towards Vasily. I wanted to show the new Zahir a picture of what he would look like in six months, save him a nervous breakdown. And that suit at the same time.

'You want me to pull rickshaw out of my ass, Arman?' Vasilly shouted. 'Where do you see spare rickshaw for him, where? You tell me and I will rent it to him.'

But there *were* spare rickshaws, lots of them. Lithuanians had brought a hundred over from Poland. They were being rented out as fast as they could be assembled. The likes of the new Zahir and the international students were lining up for them down outside the Lithuanian's enclosure.

'Give him Irish's rickshaw,' Arman said. 'He doesn't even pay rent!'

I flash-boiled. I hated every single square inch of the cube-headed bastard with all my raging heart. I got right up in his face and he got right up in mine. Our foreheads touched and our thoughts and dreams were separated by nothing but some grease, grit and a bit of skull. He was nothing like me. We kept clenched fists at our side, understanding that the first to raise a hand against the other was the attacker and after that it was just self-defence.

He reached for my throat and I reached for his, both of us trying to squeeze the life out of the other until Vasily and the new Zahir broke it up.

I restarted, having lost it, chasing it now.

Rickshaws packed three deep outside the theatres, the first of them arriving a full hour before curtain-down so as to get prime position by the stalls exit. Rickshaws were planted outside every pub in Covent Garden and waited by the maps at all of the Circuses. They prowled down all the good streets. My lucky spot, the Seven Dials roundabout, was a carcass, hunted into extinction, rickshaws buzzing around it like flies. As soon as a face showed a lost expression, a swarm formed, undercutting one another in price.

'There used to be respect in this fucking business,' shouted Martha. 'Now everyone's undercutting and bickering. Fucking Lithuanians flooding the market.'

The narrow passage from Cambridge Circus onto Old Compton Street jammed. Two rickshaws at loggerheads became a regular occurrence as both riders claimed right of way, refusing to reverse to allow the other cycle on. They stood on their pedals staring into the other's eyes, interrupted only by the newbies who stopped to ask where exactly Piccadilly Circus was located, Norwegian couples in their back seats looking as bewildered as the newbie.

I restarted, the feeling slightly muddled, fighting hard to keep it.

The G-A-Y crowd wanting to go down to Heaven at Charing Cross at eleven.

I restarted, good type of numb again, back on top.

This was the time of night for learning on one's feet, tapping into the city's life force because it was a living, breathing thing that changed by the day that had mood swings and celebrations, victories and losses.

Before the pubs closed, the mulleted Colombians, a splinter Colombian group, parked up at Priscilla and shared out Chinese food given out by the buffets at the end of the night. The Bangladeshis had a contact in the cinema and they parked up, dipping their arms into a giant bin liner full of popcorn, fisting the stuff into their mouths. I couldn't remember if I had eaten. I didn't feel hungry.

I restarted, losing it a bit, needing a fare quickly.

I cycled on, smashing an energy drink before the *where's open?* crowd started. My knee stung now and my eyeballs caked over with rust, a pain in my arm as I pedalled over to Islington with two guys who told me to just follow a rickshaw of girls on up ahead—*catch them, mate, catch them. Oi, oi—where you off to tonight ladies?*

I restarted.

Bertie was inside the Paradise Gaming Hall pouring pound coins into the one-arm bandits. He had pedalled all day for watermelons, cherries and sevens, all of which were not lining up. His rickshaw was parked outside, six Swedish flags attached to it now so as to attract the Swedes.

June came and went.

I restarted.

I got three guys from a stag party plus the dwarf that was passed out and handcuffed to the stag, being cradled in his arms like a baby. The dwarf moaned, tearing away at his skin suit.

'Leave it on, fella, good lad,' said the stag. 'Oh Jesus Christ, I think he's shat himself—ah fuck sake. He has—the fuckin dwarf's shat himself.'

It spread around to the other rickshaws that the dwarf had shat himself. There was a cheer.

'Right let's get this started,' said the leader. 'All rickshaws in a line please. First down gets fifty pounds—all other positions get zip. On your marks, oi—get back there—get set—the smell of that dwarf is rank—go!'

We whizzed and whipped through traffic, coming through and finding spaces where spaces should not have been, edging out, elbowing in. Their hotel came into view. We pushed hard. The passengers roared. I couldn't think about anything but the turn of the pedal, the push, the trail, and the doing it all over again, steaming, huffing and wheezing my way towards the hotel, cramping and spasming, fighting on inside a terrified and trembling body, grinding out cartilage in my knee, irrevocably damaging my lower back, straining my heart harder and harder for the turn of the wheel, bulldozing my way through the lot of it.

I restarted.

It was July and hot. London was in drought, the reservoirs low and bottled water prices high. The clubs down on Leicester Square boiled, the nights all named on their flyers—*Furnace* Friday, Saturday *Inferno. Blaze* mid-week specials. The ice trucks rolled in because the club's ice machines were not hacking the pace. The buildings ran out of sweat and started to melt. The stench of burning stone and tar mixed with the stink of piss. The streets scooched tighter, the cabbies raged, rattling around in their sweltering little cabs like bottled wasps, revving their bumpers closer and closer and closer. Death by black cab was as readily available as a Big Mac and only riders with hummingbird hearts were making it.

The girl in her knickers was maybe twenty years old. She stumbled in front of me. Her knickers were black and lacy and she was wearing only an extra small glittery t-shirt to cover the rest. Some of the crowd took out their camera phones.

'Jesus Christ, is that the fashion now? Just going out in your pair of knickers?' someone said.

The girl in her knickers fell and the camera phones surrounded her like mantling hawks.

A sensible, mid-size, family saloon car came to our flank. Homemade rap and weed fumes flooded out the windows. The exhaust was getting revved ridiculously. Four young men sat in each corner of the car, pierced with diamond earrings, scrawled with neck and knuckle tattoos, sporting either flat-caps or razor-designed hair. The driver leaned out his window and begun a conversation with the girl in her knickers. I cycled over.

'You got us stoppin' traffic and that,' the boy racer was saying. 'Come on, jump in, we'll take you home, no worries, sweetheart.'

'Why you wanna go home so early?' said someone in the back of the car.

The girl in her knickers slumped against a window ledge not knowing what was going on, long strands of wet hair matting down the side of her face.

'Come on, I know boys will be boys and that,' said the boy racer. 'But it ain't that. Hop in.'

I pulled up beside the girl in her knickers. 'Get on,' I said, motioning my head towards the backseat, telling her it was the boy-racer or me. 'It's fine. You'll be safe.'

She slumped aboard.

'I have no money,' she said.

'It's fine. Don't worry. Where do you live?'

'Waterloo.'

'You can have the bitch,' the boy-racer said and sped away angry.

I cycled on with the girl in her knickers in the backseat.

Three boys were projectile vomiting outside Charing Cross Station when we were passing. The vomit was the colour pink. It landed all around them in a soupy splatter and the boy's heads, chests and arms were covered in the stuff.

'That's foul,' said a face in the crowd. 'They must've been spiked.'

'Hey,' I called over to them from the side of the street. 'Where do you all live?'

'North Peckham,' one of them managed to say.

'Get in,' I told them.

'I eat men like air,' said the girl in her knickers and wrapped herself around the side of the backseat to make room for the boys who were making their way over on their hands and knees.

'We have no money,' said the first boy to arrive.

'Just make sure and vomit off the side,' I told him, pulling him up and on.

The second arrived and I pulled him up. The third managed it on his own, pink dribbling down from his chin.

'You all have sick on you,' said the girl in her knickers.

I cycled on, catching a nice breeze up the Strand, the backseat quiet as we crossed Waterloo Bridge, me pedalling extra fast across it just in case the girl in her knickers had mermaid ambitions. A light easterly wind came across the Thames and cooled our faces. There was a statue of Atlas with the world on his shoulders for the mythology exhibition at the Royal Festival Hall. Atlas himself was unimpressive as an idea to me though. The girl in her knickers called all the men in the world wankers. One of the boys wretched like he was trying to expel a lung up through his throat. Atlas carried the planet. I carried its people.

'Pussy,' I whispered over to him.

The sun was still underground but threatened to rise any second. I dug hard to try and beat it, to get the stranded home before it did. It was a fight between us. I hated it and felt it hated me. Once the sun was up, the tube reopened, the day buses got going again, the fresh cabbies started their day's work and people did not have to get a rickshaw and were too sober to be seen on one. When I saw it rising, I felt defeat, the same defeat that the four horses of Helios had suffered centuries before. I needed the night-time stranded and when the sun had risen, I felt bronzed, turned into a statue, pinned by a big fat finger to the ground and left furious and angry, frozen and stopped until night fell once again.

'Just these apartments here,' said the girl in her knickers. I pulled up to her front door and the girl in her knickers hopped out and walked away.

'Was she in her knickers?' asked one of the boys.

I cycled on, through mute streets, down past Elephant and Castle hitting the New Kent Road. The three boys got hit by a second wave of sickness and leaned their heads over the side of the rickshaw in preparation.

'No,' I shouted through the pain and sweat and gritted teeth. 'You can walk.' 'Us?' asked one of the boys.

'No, not you,' I said.

The sun was starting to rise and I pedalled harder to get the beating of it.

The day started again and I pedalled right into it.

I couldn't remember when sleep became only four hours a night. Then three. Then none.

I restarted.

A thousand naked people on bikes gathered at Hyde Park Corner. The naked rubbed themselves with lotion to avoid sore burns on sensitive areas. There were small, athletic types of breasts and enormous engorgements. There were neat, prim vaginas and big, bushy ones that looked like Predator from the film. There were monstrous horse-dicks and growers-not-showers, arses that needed two seats on a plane and others as small as summer peaches. There were the half-hearted, too—women who left their bras on and men not parting with their underpants. There were naked men who wore gorilla masks to hide their identity. I guess they wanted to feel wind around their balls but did not want their boss to see both their face and wind-strewn balls together in the *Metro* on Monday morning.

'God, I hope none of my students are here,' said a naked woman on rollerblades, affixing a pink wig while taking cover behind my rickshaw from the sleazy men with cameras. 'I have to do it though, I mean, it's not everyday you get a chance to roller-blade naked through Central London, is it?'

Imrus came to my side, naked except for his footwear that did not match. On the left foot was a pink trainer, on the right was a brown shoe—no socks.

'My wife's family. They steal my shoes and socks,' he said. 'You have customer yet, Irish?'

'Not yet,' I said, trying not to look at little Imrus.

'You are afraid to be naked?'

'No, not afraid. Just not much point.'

'It helps you get a fare if you are naked. People are afraid to be with rider with

clothes on. It scares them.'

I hopped off the saddle and stripped, putting my clothes underneath the backseat. Imrus looked me up and down.

'I remember when you were a fat bastard, Irish,' he said.

I took a look at myself. There was not a pick of fat on me. I was ripped—enormous steel thighs and a rock hard stomach.

'Good man,' Imrus said and turned and walked over to clothed people, asking if they wanted a ride. He looked like one of those wrinkled dogs—the Shar-pei—his comb over blowing in the wind. The clothed shied away from his offer but grabbed at their cameras when he had passed. He looked mental.

The naked got the last of the slogans painted on their backs. There was stuff like, *One less car* and

Ban engines in Central London and *60 cyclists killed on London roads every year.*

'Excuse me, are you free?' said a girl with an American accent. 'Could you take us in this naked ride? How much would you charge?'

'It's free.'

'Cool,' she said. Her boyfriend arrived and they both got naked, giggling to themselves. They had tattoos all over their legs, chests, arms and backs. The boyfriend had a sword tattooed on his dick. Normal penises had one dangle. This monstrosity had two or three dangles. They sat up on the backseat and the sleazy photographers swarmed around us and started to snap pictures.

'I'm Sarah. This is Eric.'

'I'm Irish.'

'Riders get ready,' shouted the steward. 'Please, move back photographers and let the riders pass. Please move back.'

The photographers moved back but only a little bit. More and more of the clothed disrobed in the final minute, flash-stripping and packing away clothes in baskets and backpacks. The start was a gauntlet of perverts, photographers and religious protesters. The Holy Joes had set up on the footpath with blankets at hand for any of the naked that saw the light and wanted to cover up.

'Weren't Adam and Eve naked?' Sarah shouted.

'You preposterous people,' the protestor shouted back. 'Jerusalem hath grievously sinned; therefore she is removed: all that honoured her despise her, because they have seen her nakedness: yea, she sigheth, and turneth backward.'

'Whatever,' shouted Eric.

'What you are doing, sir—is meaningless,' shouted a religious protestor into his little megaphone. 'Shame on you.'

The protestors had heaven in fifty or sixty years to keep them going. They were sure of it. The naked were not sure of anything and just wanted a little bit of happiness now. They were not ashamed. Neither was I. We felt we were telling the world that we were there—that we were human—flesh and bone. I smiled at the Holy Joes and forgave them. It must have been tough having to be anti-everything all the time, begrudging in the name of love. The Holy Joes smiled back because I was going to Hell.

We lined up in one long row. There were naked people on tandem bikes, naked people on unicycles, naked people on skateboards, naked people on roller-skates. There were naked joggers and naked people on penny-farthings, and about fifteen hundred other naked people on bicycles, all in body-paint and masks, sprayed with glitter, beaming nude, and proud. The sun was shining and everybody was happy. Bells chimed. The Americans in the backseat cheered and hooted. The Naked Bike Ride began. We moved on, two thousand happy and naked people rolling down Piccadilly. Shop owners threw out chocolate bars and drinks, people cheered and young boys all looked grateful for the biology lesson. Sometimes, people just needed a laugh. Naked people on bikes were funny.

For a moment I felt free amongst the guys pulling wheelies, girls on rollerblades and elderly couples on tandem bikes, and the smiles and the happiness. I forgot about trying to get fares and competing with other riders. I felt myself as though riding a normal bicycle, naked and carefree. I imagined pulling wheelies on an empty street without a backseat full of stranded people.

'Dude, you OK?' asked Eric.

'Yes,' I said.

'You've been talking to yourself for like five minutes. I mean it was funny I guess for the first minute or so, but now you're kinda freakin' us out.'

'Sorry.'

Imrus passed me with a lone naked gentleman in his backseat, trying to take a picture of himself naked with 10 Downing Street in the background.

The naked moved on down Whitehall, past Big Ben and over Westminster Bridge. I could not get the wish of not having a backseat out of mind. I wished for a normal bike to pull wheelies with, normal acceleration and braking, normal pedal resistance, normal steering.

'You're like, falling behind,' Sarah said.

The street was back to normal, still with the fizz of commotion about, but normal. The traffic was moving, the buses passing. The crowds on the footpaths had dispersed. The traffic all looked at us. The buildings stared. The sunlight roasted my back.

There was an ambulance up ahead putting the teacher on rollerblades into the back. She had hurt her leg but was trying to tell the police to calm down. They were berating the Turkish rider, Kudret who looked genuinely sorry for causing the accident. He apologized to the girl on rollerblades. She told him not to worry.

'You're not the one who would have to make the phone call to a family home to tell them their daughter has been killed. Are you? You know what that's like?' said one of the policemen. Kudret was then arrested, handcuffed and sat in the back of his own rickshaw, still naked.

I braked. I was not getting the Americans home. I was only bringing them in one big circle of the city.

'OK, guys. I got to go,' I said.

'Seriously?' asked Sarah.

'I'm sorry.'

The Americans hopped off and we all got dressed like it was the morning after. They hated me— thought I was a weirdo. I just didn't want to see the expressions on two thousand people's faces when they had to put their clothes back on, and realised that naked was not enough.

The naked Kudret rolled past us on the backseat of his own rickshaw, his hands cuffed behind him, a policeman pedalling him to Charing Cross Police Station.

'You are a fuck. A stupid fuck,' Kudret was roaring, kicking his own rickshaw.

'Keep talking,' said the policeman over his shoulder. 'See what happens.'

Imrus pedalled in chase, the naked man befuddled in the backseat. 'This stupid law is for horses,' Imrus shouted. 'Let him go. It is my wife's family behind all of this.'

'I'm remembering you,' replied the policeman, trying to keep his eyes on the road in front and maintain authority but unsure of dimension and steering, a face on him like a nervous newbie.

'Fuck,' roared Kudret, distracting him further.

'Let him go,' shouted Imrus.

'Both of you shut up or see what happens,' shouted the policeman.

I cycled on.

I needed a fare—'Lift there, folks?'

I restarted.

Vasily was calling for his money.

I restarted.

Down from Leicester Square, the cops had brought in an articulated mobile processing unit and cordoned off the square at the junction of Orange and Irving. Undercover policemen walked the streets. 'Strip club, mate? Know any strip clubs?' the undercovers asked riders. The trap was that a rider might backtrack and therefore be cycling the wrong way down a one way for which they could be arrested and the rickshaw confiscated under the newly dusted off law. It was always two big men dressed smart casual with freshly washed, stain-free jeans. They faked hiccups like a child would act drunk, and stopped to press a shoulder against a wall or pretend to check out a public map, all of it as fake-casual as their clothes. They were too sharp, too interested in the street, and there was a bulge in their clothes where the walkie-talkie, search gloves and handcuffs were being kept.

The thing was, it really didn't matter how good you were at spotting them. The trouble was, they walked around corners at any given moment, catching riders taking a shortcut over a footpath or a quick shoot down a one-way. Then they broke smart character and said, *Hold it there, fella.*

Riders who had accepted their wrongdoing and gave no aggro, waited outside the mobile processing unit for their rickshaw confiscation slips. The arresting undercover would come out of the mobile processing unit and hand them the summons and court date.

'There's guys selling smack up on Gerrard Street,' the riders all said.

'We have a team working on that, too,' said the undercovers.

The riders who didn't accept it as well as these guys, the bad 'uns like Kudret, went to the cop shop for an etiquette lesson.

The undercovers were no good for anyone. Riders were bringing them to the After Parties and it all had to close. The line of shops down from Leicester Square that were fronts for drug dealing told all the young guys showing up for work to go home, that it was too hot around. The young guys who tried to go it alone and sell a bit themselves were slapped about by the shop assistants or hauled away in the Paddy Wagons with the bag snatchers.

I restarted. I'd worry about it later.

And then pedalling all started to feel like a fall.

I could not remember when I first slipped.

I could not remember when it all got bad and then got worse.

I could not even remember how long I had been falling. Hours span on into days that span on into months that span around and around.

I restarted.

It was August.

I restarted.

'Come and get me,' my father had said the night he died.

'No. I've had enough of this,' I said.

'Fair enough. I'll just go and kill myself then.'

'Why do you say that stuff?'

'I'm tired of it all.'

'You're a coward.'

'Come and get me.'

'No. You can walk.'

I had sat at the kitchen table all night waiting for him, practicing talking some sense into him, trying to work out the perfect piece of reason that would bring an end to the madness and the addiction and the turmoil, practicing talking him into life. Then the doorbell rang. I looked at the clock on the kitchen wall. It was nearly six in the morning. I walked out into the hallway and opened the front door. It was the police, hats in hand.

I needed a fare.

The Tricycle

The passenger in the car was a woman, looking just about there, as in, she looked like women looked on television, sweat all running down their faces, four minutes away from having a baby, panic stations all-round. The driver reached across the woman's belly and opened the passenger door.

'Get out,' he shouted.

And then I realised that it was Marie.

And that I was dreaming.

She got out of the car and stood there on the street looking four minutes off, and this guy, the driver, drove away down Martins Lane. Marie looked alone in his wake, stranded and crying. A crowd then formed around her and asked her things. She said things back and they all put their hands to their mouths in shock.

I floated over to the crowd and someone said she should lie down in the back seat where she would be more comfortable until the ambulance arrived.

'I could bring her down to the hospital?' I said.

'No, far too dangerous on that thing. Just please, let her lie down on the back and wait for the ambulance.'

'Christ, anything,' Marie said, grabbing hold of my handlebar to wear down a contraction. She did not know it was me, or maybe, I thought, she had forgotten me.

'OK. Come on, get her up.'

I helped her on board by her elbows and wrists. She slumped across the back, held her belly and opened her legs wide.

'Try not to think about it,' I said.

'Try not to think about what? The human being coming out of my vagina? When I'm done here, I'm shovin' a watermelon up your arse—then I'm gonna say—try not think about it. Then we'll fucking see.'

'You've got a mouth on you.'

'And?'

'And I like it.'

'I hate men,' she screamed, half laughing, half crying.

'What's your name?'

'Marie.'

'Well, my name's Irish. An ambulance is on the way.'

'Too late, too late. It's too late. It's coming.'

'No, stop, wait.

'I fucking well can't, can I?'

'Who was the car? The guy in the car? Who was the guy in the car?'

'Vasily,' Marie said. 'That was Vasily.'

'Why'd he drive off?'

'I told him he's not the father.'

The crowd gasped like it was a daytime soap.

'Well, maybe you could've told him that after he had brought you to the hospital?'

'He would've known. As soon as it was born. As soon as he seen it. I couldn't do it to him. Ow, ow, ow. Jesus Christ Almighty. Better this way.'

'Better? In the back of a rickshaw? On Long Acre? Please *wait* for the ambulance.'

'I can't, I can't.'

'Please don't.'

'It's coming. Please Irish, help me. I think it's coming.'

She started to cry again. I rolled up my sleeves.

'OK, calm, calm, calm. I'm going to look. Not to be a pervert or anything. I'm just going to see if it's really coming. OK?'

'OK.'

'OK?' I asked everybody else.

'OK,' they said.

'OK,' I said and lifted her dress. It was crowning or whatever they called it, stretched and throbbing and still a vagina, Jim—but not as we know it.

'Ow, ow, ow.'

Something was there—something wet and shiny and rubbery.

'Look, stop, stop, stop,' I said, slamming back down the dress. 'OK, just stop. Wait for the ambulance.'

'Fuck you,' Marie screamed.

'It's coming. There's no doubt about that,' a woman in the crowd said who had taken a look for herself.

'You do something would you?' I asked her but she walked away like it was none of her business.

'Typical London,' a man said. I looked to *him* to take charge but he pointed to his watch then walked away, too.

'Water,' I said. 'We need water. Anyone have any water?'

I was passed water. I cracked the cap and slugged it back, taking a nice big refreshing drink and it settled me somewhat.

'OK, well if you're not going to try and wait for the ambulance,' I said, lifting back up the dress. 'Push. I suppose.'

'Really?'

'Yes, yes, push.'

Marie grit her teeth and looked like she was going for it.

'You push like a girl,' I said. 'A man would've had this out and been back to work a half hour ago.'

'Christ Almighty, shut up, Irish—ow, ow, oowww.'

I had one hand on her inside thigh to keep the legs apart and one holding her hip. I was terrified and wanted to wake up.

The crowd held its breath. The street rumbled. It was coming—coming. Then out popped a front bicycle wheel, staying there in front of us, suspended by whatever else was attached to it and still coming. I took the wheel in my hands to support it. There was nothing else to do. There were spokes, a hub and a rim, a valve and a fully inflated tyre.

'Keep pushing,' I said. There would be plenty of time for her knowing afterwards. 'You're nearly there.'

A few people blessed themselves then took off screaming up Long Acre.

'It's fine,' I told Marie. 'Everything's fine.'

'That's not right, mate,' said a banker, holding his tie against his chest while he leaned in closer with his phone to get a picture.

'Don't pay any attention to them, Marie, keep pushing.'

Marie kept pushing and out arrived a front steering column with handlebars that sprang into place as soon as they hit the outside world. Blue ribbons protruded from their end and flailed about happily. There was a little bell attached and I rang it to make sure it worked. It did. The brakes were solid and responsive, too. Marie kept pushing and out came the little crossbar, a saddle and clunky little pedals. Finally, the two back wheels sprang out and into place, as had the handlebars. The whole tricycle was out. I took a needle-nose pliers from underneath the backseat, popped the chain then clipped it back around its own chainring and cogset so that it was good to go all on its very own.

'It's a tricycle,' I said.

Marie looked like she had expected as much. 'It's yours, Irish. You're the father.'

And there it was, my child, and nothing was new.

Marie got up out of the backseat and walked away down Martin's Lane to catch the second half of Chicago.

I laid the tricycle in the backseat and took him on his first spin of the city. I pedalled with all my heart, ferociously, barbarously, unstoppable. Bricks tumbled down off the National Portrait Gallery as we passed. The lions down on Trafalgar crumbled into dust from the brisance of power exploding from my knees and calves. Nuts, washers and bolts shot from the rickshaw like cannonballs and crashed into the buildings to our either side, taking out entire wings. We flew up the Strand, tyres barely touching the surface of the road, carried along by our own velocity. A vapour cone formed on our tail and we were Mach 5, supersonic. Balls of flame burst out through the windows and onto the street below, crashing into bonnets of cars, melting through the tar and steel mesh of the street, slashing train-lines ten stories beneath. Tributaries of lead dripped off the roofs and formed a molten river in the road. Fire alarms and car alarms and burglar alarms all steamed. The crowds burst out of the theatres in panic, along with the actors and stagehands and ushers.

Buses swerved and buildings overturned. Horns glowed white and detonated like nail bombs, sprinkling shrapnel across the Lion King. The Waldorf exploded. Pigeons fell out of the sky and thumped the ground, dead and burnt.

The Thames ignited. The London Eye span so fast that the pods could not withstand the force and they were sent catapulting into the crimson sky, people becoming weightless before they met their mangled end, some in Brixton, some as far as Richmond and Kew. The trains plummeted into the depths of the Thames from Charing Cross Bridge and the passengers flung off their clothes and wildly fucked one another before imminent death. The Southbank and Royal Festival Hall veranda crowds raided abandoned bars, pouring wine, gin and beer down their necks because tomorrow there would be no hangover or consequences, having finally realised that it was all just stone and glass.

The fire brigade blew up Fulham, Kensington, Marylebone, Euston and Farringdon, all to create a firebreak but the cinders crossed in the wind and made way for the flames, the white fire too mighty, and London could not be saved.

With the world burning down around us, I pedalled on until the rickshaw frame bolts broke and the wheels warped, until the tyre air had long since seeped into the Kent countryside and the rubber had mangled and cut under the steel of the rim. Until the spokes sprung and the wheel rims became triangles that mashed and flapped and no longer turned, until the chain and crossbar snapped, until the rickshaw simply disintegrated to dust underneath my tricycle and me.

PUNCTURES

I had never seen Vasily out on the street. He lived at the base, constantly fiddling around with gears and wheels, looking for his missing ferret or demanding unpaid rent from the newbies who were not making it. But there he was, storming down through Soho Square on the back of a rickshaw shouting *faster, faster* at one of the newbies who was driving him.

'Irish, you have seen Stink?' Vasily shouted.

'No. What's going on?'

'Stink is the *going on*. If you see him, you call me immediately. If you get puncture, you call me. Let's go—go, go, go, you newbie bullshit,' Vasily mushed.

I cycled on, stopping for nothing or nobody.

Martha was in the middle of the street inspecting her back wheels. More riders were further up, inspecting their back ends, too. Traffic was held to a stop because of them. It was right before the burst of theatres at ten so everyone was anxious to get to their lucky spots. The lights turned green but nobody could move, and if there's one-thing drivers hated, it was being stopped when a green light was telling them to go. The cabbies went ballistic, trying to blow Martha and the other riders off the face of the earth.

'You all should die,' one roared out his window. 'Shot. Every last one of you.'

'You're all about as thick as the back of your own balls that have only ever seen shit,' shouted Martha.

The cabbies took time to figure out the words. Martha went back to inspecting her wheels.

Washed-up rickshaws were all down Charing Cross Road towards Leicester Square. Rickshaws were stopped dead, wheels seared, some with the valves popped off, others having been given big buckling chops, throngs of riders beginning the lug back to base. It was full metal puncture, riders fighting one another, blaming those few still rolling for their slashed wheels, or blaming faces in the crowd, or threatening black cab drivers who were threatening back—the enemy all around yet nowhere to be seen.

Other riders were surrounded by patrol cars and community officers. They said *Stink, Stink, Stink* then stopped to watch me pass.

The little nods of acceptance had stopped. There was the question of the missing Chinese girl from the Russians, the blame for Zahir from the Bangladeshi's and the accusations of crazy carry-on from everybody—talking to myself and howling and so on. Even Gunda had stopped chatting to me since Arman told everyone I was giving free lifts. I could feel the animosity pressing down on me with the dirty looks.

I used the hill to fly down to the National Portrait Gallery and hung a left onto the path, around the Big Issue headquarters and across the cobbles down to Charing Cross station, not stopping for lights, pegging it up the Strand and cutting down to Adam Street where it was dark and nobody was around, where breath was the loudest thing. It was a place to bring rolled up carpets and men in cement booths, the river somewhere over the parapet in the blackness below.

I reached under my backseat for an energy drink. I had been buying them by the crate.

'Can I've one?' came a voice from the shadows.

He was halfway down a flight of steps, a samurai sword resting on his toes, its point being dug into the wall, putting the finishing touches to a big *S*. There was a hill to contend with—an escape was unlikely if he chose to chase with the sword.

'If you stay away from my tyres with that sword you can,' I said.

'A deal, sir. Well brokered.'

'Here,' I said, throwing one down to him. The can burst off the corner of a step and fizzed all the way down into the blackness.

'My coordination's not up to its usual Olympic standard. Could you perhaps pass me an elixir, sir?'

I got another and stepped off.

'Could you put down that sword if I'm going down there?'

'I must refer you to the deal, sir and remind you there was nothing about disarmament.'

He was starting with a *T* to follow the *S*, scratching the tip of the blade into the wall.

'Just take it easy,' I said.

'I am perfectly fine.'

'There're a few guys around tonight who'd like to change that,' I said, leaning down to him, stretching the can as far as my fingers could reach, out of sudden-chop radius.

'Sycophants and connivers. Deserve it. Never trust a Russian. Never a Russian. No indeed,' said Stink, reaching for the can. The underside of his forearm was covered with punctured sores. Some were festered, others scabbed. Then his face came into the light. He had been beaten. Both cheeks were huge and the eyes inside them were purple and sad. There were cuts and scrapes across his forehead and his lip was burst in half. 'You should see the other—I made short work of his fist. The very butcher of a fist is I.'

His can tisked. He gulped at it until it was a scrunched-up empty then threw it towards the river. 'Did you know a goat herder in Ethiopia noticed that when his goats ate from a certain bush they became enlivened and frisky, jumping about, full of energy?'

'I did not.'

'It would have been fine but then the goat herder ate some and he felt the same—all energized and good-to-go. He told the monks about it and they made a drink from it. Magic beans they called them.

Magic beans. Bouncing goats are all well and good on magic beans but infuse those good-to-go goats with hope-filled souls and that sir, is a dangerous animal.'

'How did you manage to walk around slashing all those tyres with that?'

'Popcorn addicts and ice-cream eaters just pop up out of the ground and then when the job's done they scurry back down their holes. Popping up. Scurrying back down. Popping up, back down. Up, down.' His finger demonstrated the difference between the two words.

'Do you want a lift? If not, I've got to go, Stink.'

'Before you go, perhaps you could leave me with one more of your delicious libations?'

I took out another can and rolled it down the steps to him. He stopped it and raised it into the air between two fingers.

'Behold, our destruction,' he said, opening the can and slugging it back in one.

'All of the coffee shops and the pubs and the sex houses. What are they all evolving towards? The shops, these emotion and energy shops that sell instant determination and extra strength focus and bottled energy—in the—the, the future, what will they become?'

'One shop.'

'Forget shops. Further down the road than one shop.'

'I don't know, Stink.'

'A pill. One single pill. A daily pill for life that we line up for at the start of every day. The God pill. To compete you see. Because we invented the machine and now we have to compete with it. You see? One single pill. A dozen billion little machines going up and down, up and down, up and down. Yes, sir. Indeed—one pill. A dangerous animal. All because we were trying to find the wherewithal. The coffee shops into energy shops to wherewithal pills. Little machines huddled into megacities, wanting more than the real world, because it's not enough. The real world is not enough so vendors roll their carts of numbness about the streets, selling to a population that wants heightened elation forever, all of the moments all at once, wrapping themselves up cosy inside their very own tailored-heaven, God no longer good enough as he's now an aspiration, see? A dozen billion superhuman perfect little machines with prosthetic enhancements, wheels for legs and tungsten hearts, creating themselves in the image of machines because the sun will eventually die and if they can out-pedal it, if they could just out-pedal it.'

Stink started to boil and twitch, and click his fingers beside his ears like he was testing sound was still there.

'I've got to go,' I said.

Stink stood up on guard with the sword. 'Apothecary—I remember our negotiation and I will honour it. No slashing of the tyres in exchange for your magic beans,' Stink said, climbing the steps as would a Samurai with both hands gripping the sword by his side. He bent over my front wheel. 'But you said nothing about a kiss.'

He leaned in and kissed the rubber with his scabbed lips.

'Know your enemy, you see? Know your enemy.'

A shout came from the top of the street. 'What the Hell?'

It was Imrus.

'You, Irish! You are with Stink and my wife's family. You are sabotaging me.'

'Relax, Imrus,' I said.

'You are trying to puncture me, Irish!'

'I'm not trying to puncture you, Imrus!'

Stink ran towards the parapet and leaped over it, wielding the sword high above his head, landing somewhere in the dark and out of sight, maybe in the trees, maybe in the Thames with the mermaids.

Imrus pedalled away shouting that I was in cahoots with Stink. I could feel my days of a rider numbered and it terrified me.

The Straight Jacket

There was a story I told passengers on long jour-
neys, when the lights and buzz of the West End
had drizzled away behind us, and in the silence I
could hear them think, *perhaps we've made a mistake—
this is taking too long—I'm bored. Maybe we should just get
him to pull over and we'll get a cab the rest of the way?*

'When Louis IX of France heard that the King
of England was starting a zoo,' I'd say, 'He sent him
an elephant as a present. I don't know if it was a joke
or what, because nobody in England had ever seen
an elephant at that time. Maybe Louis knew it would
confuse the bejesus out of the English and had a
right laugh with his courtiers about it. But anyway,
people flocked from all over the place just to see
this elephant that they kept down at the Tower of
London. There were three lions there and a polar
bear from the King of Denmark and monkeys and
an ostrich. The king was building up quite the collection. But it was possibly the worst zoo in history.
The lions regularly mauled people, a leopard actually ripped off a woman's arm down there, the ostrich

died from eating steel nails because people thought ostriches ate metal, the polar bear was swimming in the moat that was filled with the most vilest disease-ridden filth and shit imaginable. And the zebra was in the canteen with the Beefeaters everyday, drinking beer with them. And then there's this elephant. And nobody knows what to feed it. It's not like they could just Google it, you know? So they put this big barrel of red wine in front of it, and a big slab of beef. And the elephant's like, eh, what the fuck, lads? I'm an elephant—I eat grass n' shit.

'But day in, day out, for two years, the Beefeaters keep putting red wine and beef in front of him for dinner. And the elephant has no choice because he's chained up and living in this tiny little box they made for him, you know? It wasn't like he could just saunter on down to the shops and buy himself a bunch of bananas. So he just drinks and drinks and drinks for two years, until he dies. And that's the story of the drunken elephant in the Tower. And you can imagine everyone finally standing around this dead elephant saying, the drink finally caught up with him.'

'So they killed the elephant?' the passengers would say.

'Yeah,' I'd say.

'That's a horrible story.'

The elephant in the Tower came to mind when the hands came out of the crowd, sharp and quick, at least two pairs that held the brakes down and grabbed me.

Beside me, the horses of Helios were reared up out of the fountain on their hind legs with more gusto than usual, the four of them trying to get away from the ground as fast as they could. I should have known something was about. If any horses were to know something, these would be the horses.

I imagined what the elephant must have thought when he was over in France, having a right time eating crunchy hay, drinking mountain-spring water then all of a sudden he's seized and bundled off to festering London, not knowing what was going on.

I thought I was being robbed. I lashed out, strong and fierce, grabbed a body by the scruff and landed him a head-butt. My forehead cut on his teeth and blood spouted down into my eyes. I couldn't see so I was just lashing out at anything that touched me. Someone may have said *police* but that's what I wanted at that very moment, hoping some were around to stop me from being robbed.

A knee came down on my back and squeezed the wind out of me, handcuffs were clamped on and I knew I was fucked. Had they just announced themselves, said who they were. They messed up. Not me. Yes, I broke a red. Yes, I resisted. But assault on a Constable in execution of his duty was serious. That was a custodial sentence and pleading in court that I didn't know he was a police officer didn't matter.

'Charge?' asked the Desk Sergeant down at Charing Cross Police Station. The telly was on in the corner showing *Boxing's Most Memorable Moments*. Jack

Dempsey was knocking the seven shades of shite out of Jess Willard back in 1919.

'Endangering Public Safety. Resisting arrest. Might do him on assault on a PO, too—have to see what Nichols wants to do about it,' said Constable Upton.

'Name.'

'He doesn't have one. The man with no name we've got here.'

'Name?'

'Fuck you,' I said and Upton smacked me across the head and shot me one in the ribs.

'Let's try this again,' said the Sergeant. 'Name?'

'Honestly lads, my name's *Fuck*. Surname, *You*.'

Smack. Smack. Smack.

'Did he have anything on him?'

'A phone. No wallet.'

'Well, try a number would you? Throw the little cunt into seventeen until we find out.'

On the telly, Willard finally dropped to the canvas. He was cooked. The other cops around all agreed with the Desk Sergeant that them were the glory days of boxing. When men were men.

'Come on, little cunt. You heard him. You fuckin' stink you little fuckin' pikey bastard. Go on, refuse to take your shoes and belt off. I *want* you to refuse.'

'You're as bad as your mother,' I said. 'Bitch loves it rough, too.'

Smack. Smack. Smack.

'Oh, yes, Mrs Upton. Yes, yes!'

I heard a vein pop in Upton's temple. He was one of those lads in school that started crying and trying to kill you if you mentioned their mother, breast-fed until he was ten or something, a pretty-boy, waxed-up hair like a burlesque freak-show. He regularly visited sunbeds judging by the weird-coloured tan on him. He wore a tight designer t-shirt with Japanese tattoos that reached just below the sleeve. I could see why he was chosen for undercover duty. You'd never ever think he was police, a fact I was sure the other cops reminded him of all the time which is why he was so ready to prove himself with all of the smacking and rabbit punching. He ripped my shoes and belt off, opened the cell door, unlocked the handcuffs and forced me inside with a kick to the back. The door locked and Upton said through the tray slot, 'We'll break you,' and just stood watching me in my dirty sock feet until the Desk Sergeant shouted, 'Are you making that call or just going to stand there watching him?'

The tray slot banged shut.

The cell was a nightmare—four white walls with nothing inside them but what I was thinking. I was better off handcuffed with Upton taking out his childhood issues on me. The natural order of things had stopped. The moving forwards, mornings, after-noons, nights, pedalling on and on—it had all been suspended. The beginning and end of each day had become like the beginning and end of time itself, and now in the cell, there was no time, no forwards, only one elongated *now*. How long had it been before the elephant broke inside his little box down at the Tower? Until he was a feckless, caged and drunken beast that turned carnivore and raged the wrong way up a one-way until it broke him.

'Come and get me,' my father said.

'Lift tonight, folks?' I shouted, trying to drown him out.

'Come and get me,' he said again.

I began to run in circles around the cell. 'Where you off to tonight, guys? They're not expensive, I'll do you a good price. A pound, I'll do it for a pound, sir? Right so, hop on. Where we off to? Milton Keyes, no worries, away we go. So what did you guys get up to tonight? Dinner and a show, yeah? Very nice. Very nice. Eh, it'll take about eight hours to get to Milton Keyes. Don't worry, ever hear about the elephant in the Tower? The King of England was starting a zoo, right...'

'Joe-y, oh, Joe-Joe,' shouted Upton from out in the hallway. A wrap on the door, and, 'Oh, Joooooo-seph.' It opened and in came a smiling Upton. I kept running in small circles, imagining I was on a steep incline somewhere on the way to Milton Keyes. 'It's a small, small world, Joe. I say it everyday and nobody believes me. Just off the phone with Niamh. We go way back. I broke her in, can you believe that? Tight little pussy on her back then. Don't know about now, with the kids and all that. Christ, I had that bitch squealing back in the day.'

I whacked him one in the gob, not breaking rhythm with my circling.

Upton left and came back with reinforcements.

Punches came from all around as I was taken down. I grabbed out and tried to take as many punchers as I could when I fell. Upton's face was everywhere. One of him had taken a hold of my arm and was an inch away from breaking it. Cardboard cutout cabbies then stormed the cell, all of them with balding, egg-shaped cabbie-heads, tattoos on their forearms and toothy smiles, fifty bottled wasps unbottled, raving about the way it was in them days and how things should've been done in the first place. And about how hanging wouldn't be good enough for the likes of me. They were right and everyone else was wrong. I guess it came from spending year after year in the driving seat, where passengers had to listen and agree in order to get to their destination. They helped the Upton's hold me down and give me a good Jack Dempsey going-over. Stink came in with his samurai sword atop the drunken elephant, puncturing prams and buggies and tricycles, mopeds, cars and kiddie-wagons, wheelchairs and hearses, deflating the whole world, chop by chop. It was all beautiful and chaotic and then black and soft until I regained consciousness.

'Oi,' the Desk Sergeant said, nudging me with his foot.

'You want a lift?' I asked him.

'You're owed a phone call.'

I phoned Martha. 'Who's the arresting officer? Upton or Summers? Or the new guy, Nichols?'

'Upton. But Nichols was there. I didn't know they were cops.'

'What happened?'

'I head-butted Nichols. I think he lost a tooth. I'm fucked, yeah?'

'No. You're not. Actually Irish, you have to be the luckiest bastard I've ever met in my life. I'm on my way.'

A half an hour later I was standing outside Charing Cross police station.

'Thanks, Benny,' Martha said to Upton as he held the door for us.

'It's Constable Upton.'

'Course it is, Sweetcheeks,' Martha said and pinched his arse.

He shut the door and there we were.

I could make no sense of the streets on foot. They blurred around me like spinning spokes. I looked to the tops of the buildings to try and get my bearings but it all looked the same. Every road could have led anywhere.

There was a recovery vehicle parked up outside, it's load—rickshaws, maybe ten or twelve of them all upright on their back-ends, front wheels reaching up into the night sky, the police compound full up, its driver nowhere to be seen.

My rickshaw was on it. There were no cops around, only empty cop cars.

'Thank you, Martha.'

'Irish, if you could see yourself, mate.'

'I'll get it together.'

My phone buzzed. It was Vasily. 'Where you is?' he said, sounding calm.

'I'm in the middle of a fare here, Vasily.'

'Irish. Bullshit. You is arrested.'

'I'm not. I'm out on the street.'

'Enough bullshit. Martha told me. You are making me very stressed. The police, the head guy of the London Cabs, everyone is looking for you.'

'Don't worry, Vasily,' I said.

'All that is OK. I don't give a shit about that bullshit. Yuri wants to speak with you, Irish.'

There was a silence.

'When Yuri will find you he is going to cut off your hands,' he said.

'And,' I said, not knowing what else to say.

'And leave. Get out of here. But I want my rickshaw.'

'You don't deserve it,' I said and hung up.

I turned to Martha. 'You told Vasily!'

'Irish, you're played out, man. You don't take days off, you're getting weird—it's bad, for everyone. There's non-stop complaints and now you're head-butting cops. As though the cabbies don't have enough on us. Yes, I called Vasily. You're finished and that's it. It's tough love and you need it.'

I grabbed at my hair, frightened, terrified even. Without my rickshaw I would have to get on with things, other things, what things exactly I didn't know. It was less terrifying back in the cell.

'Find something else, Irish. That's it.'

'Like what?' I said.

Martha's phone rang. 'Hey, Vasily,' she said. 'I'm down at Charing Cross Station with him now.'

I looked at my rickshaw up on the recovery lorry like I was a ghost in a film looking at his body after he had just died, not yet understanding that he was a ghost even though nobody could see him anymore or hear what he was saying and traffic was driving through him. The rickshaw was a clunky looking thing with enough dents, tears and battle scars for a battalion of rickshaws but without it, I had nothing in common with London, or the people in it. Without it, I had no confidence, no spark, no cutting edge. Without my rickshaw there was only me. There was no wheels, no go, no reason. I thought about tomorrow and about what I would do once I woke up. And what I would do then. And then after that. And then the day after.

'I'll never go back,' my father had said when he got out of alcohol rehabilitation centre up in Dublin. 'That's me finished with all that. I'll never take a drink again.'

He sat at home like he was reborn. His skin was clear, his hair brushed, his shirt ironed. We made cups of tea.

'If I could take it all back I would,' he said. 'It was a dark time and I didn't know what I was doing. I couldn't think. I'm sorry.'

I forgave him, told him everything was going to be fine.

'Thank you,' he said.

Later on in the afternoon he shifted about in his seat. His hands did not know how to sit. His eyes did not know what to look at. 'Do we need milk?' he asked. He walked to the fridge to find that there was no milk left after all the tea drinking. 'Jesus Christ, is there ever any fucking milk in this house? A simple thing to remember is milk.'

He got his coat and left and I waited up for him.

'Come and get me,' he had said.

I hopped up on the back of the lorry and started to undo the straps that tied down my rickshaw.

'Irish, you need to get off that right now and get the fuck out of here,' Martha said.

'I can't,' I said. 'And don't tell me what I need to do, Martha.'

I took my rickshaw by the front wheel and rolled the two back wheels gently over the edge, trying to lower it down as carefully as I could but its weight was too much and it fell to the ground with a thump. Cops were looking out the windows. It was time to get moving.

'Irish,' Martha shouted, grabbing the rickshaw with her giant hands.

I hopped up on the saddle, fused my soul back into its lifeless frame and began to pedal but Martha held strong. 'Piss off, Martha. You can talk, can't you? All high and mighty. You freak.'

'What did you say?'

'Freak, Martha. A freak, you're a fucking freak.'

Martha was stunned and for a split second I was stunned along with her. I wanted to reach out and say how sorry I was, how I did not mean it. Then I didn't give a shit. Fuck her.

'Fine, you're on your own. I wash my hands,' she said.

Upton opened the front door of the station once again. 'Martha,' he shouted. 'He takes that and there's nothing can be done for him.'

'He's all yours,' Martha said, walking away. It was the last time I ever saw her.

Upton ran towards me.

I pushed down the pedals fast, notched up the back gears and charged onwards.

YEAR ZERO

I was a lout, a twenty-something young lad chasing the Thames on a rickshaw in the dark, a life left behind burnt to the ground.

I needed to sort something out.

I needed a break from pedalling.

My knuckles were swollen, my palms had handlebar contusions running across them, my hamstrings and quads felt whipped and beaten, my head pounded, my eyes stung, my lips were cracked and flaking, my right knee clicked and my back felt like it was being stabbed with glass.

My fingernails even hurt.

The Thames wound through dark hectares of unbanked fields and I pedalled the road alongside it. A rain fell and I sucked it from my top lip to drink. The phone began buzzing underneath the backseat. Stopped. Buzzed again. I felt the vibrations reverberate up the crossbar, through the steering column and into my arms. I ignored it and pedalled on into the night. The phone stopped and for the longest time there was only the sound of pedalling in the dark.

'A never-ending cycle,' I said, and laughed and laughed.

The bastard sun stirred. It was still underground but streaked the sky red on into the distance.

A sign for *Mt. Pleasant Pleasure Garden* came about, a place where folks once took their leisure away from the city, when there was a city. It was far too early for the shop. I needed food and coffee. There was a cycle path through the Pleasure Garden and I took it. A shampoo smell came from the hanging baskets of hyacinths. There were goldfish and carp swimming in the ponds, peacocks, rose gardens and ivy arches. My front tyre sloshed through puddles, exciting stranded tadpoles. They tailed about in frantic circles, wanting out, wanting to come with me.

'Don't worry folks, haven't crashed in hours,' I told them.

The foxes and rabbits stopped their chasing in the paddocks and hunched shoulder-to-shoulder to observe me, keeping a close eye on their cubs and kits at the same time.

'Ever been on a rickshaw before, foxes and rabbits? No? You never forget your first.'

The foxes and rabbits said nothing.

'It's innuendo,' I told them. 'Harmless innuendo. It starts the fare with light fare. You've to remember, foxes and rabbits, not everyone's as comfortable on a rickshaw as the rider, so a laugh straight away will soothe the mood and you will most certainly stand a better chance for a tip if you make jokes.'

They were not impressed. They were parents after all. Sexual innuendo from a lad cycling a rickshaw through Kent at five in the morning was weird.

'Everything needs to be taken into account about someone standing on the side of the street, foxes and rabbits—accent, haircut, clothes, the way they walk, the direction they face, sexuality, age, weight, race—all of it matters. The number of people in the group matters, as does the time of day, day of the week, the month. In this job, all of it matters. The Spanish, for example, will not ride on a rickshaw. Novices such as yourselves should look out for a girl struggling in a pair of heels and a pissed off boyfriend who can't take the slow pace anymore. It's the easiest fare you can hope for when you start out.'

They didn't like my tone but stayed put, listening to what I had to say so they could badmouth me later back in their burrows and dens.

'OK, so you're not impressed. That's fine. But put yourselves in my position—I need fares to stay going and fares depend on finding the lost—far from home, and they may very well be full of hate for the city—not an easy place, foxes and rabbits. Cold quite a lot of the time, there are the drunken girls shouting at them from the back of stretched Hummers, the club reps trying to get them inside, the con-artists trying to catch them out. Everyone wants something from them. It's not how they imagined their pleasant little city-break was going to turn out. Then along comes me, wanting to get them home when nobody else is bothering. You tell me, foxes and rabbits, who's the bad guy?'

The foxes and rabbits said nothing again. I was tired of their nonchalance. A horse came stomping towards me as I passed his field. He braked dead to get a handle on what I was then stomped to the fence separating us, got a clear view of me and took it as a challenge. He kicked up his hind legs and ran alongside me. I stood up off my saddle, dug deep, desperate to get the beating of him. My body chugged but I fought against it. The horse had speed. I dug deeper. My heart hurt and I grabbed hold of it through my chest, one arm still on the handlebars to steer. The pain was mighty and I crawled inside it, a thousand tiny tingles, champion-king of rickshaws. I smashed the horse for pace. He neighed, pissed off and cantered back to take it out on the foxes and rabbits.

'Better luck next time, horse,' I shouted back to him, feeling good, light and airy, the last man alive and loving it. I was out the other side of the Pleasure Garden, back by the river, trembling and shook, retching, crying, cycling on fast so the horse would not see. There were potholes out in the countryside and I had to keep a close eye out for them. The rickshaw felt frail and ready to fall apart. It rattled and clicked and there was a squeaking in the back wheels.

Lights switched on in houses and groggy-looking folk appeared in kitchen windows to turn on kettles. A loud engine revved behind me and changed down a gear. I thought it was a black cab and expected the worst. A horn sounded. I held on tight. A Royal Mail post truck overtook me, the driver looking at me through his passenger window, definitely not liking the cut of my jib. I was up to no good—he knew. Men in high-vis vests were overtaking me in their cars and white vans. A woman wearing white overalls and carrying a packed lunch came to the side of the road to wait for her lift to work—a painter, a neat one. No drips or smears or careless spills on her overalls. She looked up from rolling a cigarette, a filter held in her lips. Her expression told me I was the strangest thing she had ever seen.

'Need a lift?'

'No.'

And like that she was gone, behind me, forgotten.

I was so tired. Thought at that level of tiredness was razor sharp and sore. The sun was up and hurting my eyes with light and trickily shaped shadows. The phone started to buzz again. Stopped. Buzzed again.

There was a fizzy silhouette of a person on a bike through the hedge. I thought maybe it was a reflection and I wondered if leaves reflected. Then I thought about shadows but this person on a bike was in the wrong place to be a shadow.

'What are you?' I shouted.

'A man on a bike,' came the response.

'Me? Are you me?'

'No, I'm a different man on a bike. On this side of the hedge.'

He was nice and clear with his explanation. He was a man that thought about what he said and did not waste words. I liked that. I wished I could have done that. I wished I could have got to the point of things like that. The man on the bike was my new hero.

'I thought you were me and I was talking to myself.' We cycled on in peace for a minute or two. 'So,' I said finally. 'Why are you cycling in the field?'

'Too dangerous on them roads,' said the man on the bike. 'Truck ran me down a month ago.'

There were flattened hedgehogs and squashed birdies all over the road and I knew he was telling the truth. The road was starting to mean business and the white vans were in a queue behind me trying to pass. It was a tailback of about fifteen vehicles, some beeping horns, others shouting out their windows, telling me to get the fuck off the road with that piece of shit.

'What are you doing?' said the man on the bike.

'Escaping,' I said. 'Again.'

He let my answer hang for a bit.

'No matter where you go, you'll still be there.'

The field that he was cycling in was almost coming to an end. 'Do you have any food?' I asked.

'No,' said the man on the bike.

'Well, best of luck.'

'And to you.'

The main road was too busy and the horn-beeping was turning violent. I veered off into the back roads, on narrow laneways with grass growing in the middle of them and lumping big rocks on the verges. I pedalled up and down hills, beside golden fields of haystacks, through big dollops of cowshit and syca-more tree tunnels.

I wanted one more moment. The pedalling was killing me. My legs were ready to drop off but I needed the thousand tiny tingles one more time. The champion-king of rickshaws moment. I wanted it. After the next moment, I promised myself I would stop and rest. I kept cycling on, whimpering from the pain. One more moment, I thought. One more moment and that would be enough.

The road behind was the past. I knew that. The exact piece of road I was on at that very moment was the present. The road ahead was not as clear. Every direction was the same. Every road seemed the same way. Any way could have been a way. I tried to figure it out. It was the beginning all over again. Or the end all over again. The three wheels beneath me went around and around but I was sure of one thing—I was not going back.

There were combine harvesters in farmyard sheds and tasty-looking cows in the fields.

'I'm never going back,' I shouted to the cows. I wanted to eat one whole. I was so hungry. They appeared Friesian.

'You appear Friesian,' I shouted to them, and laughed and laughed and laughed. The cows didn't get it. It was all only words to them.

WHITE CLIFFS

The road I had cut Kent in half with ended at the sea, on white cliffs that stretched away out on both sides. I was stretched too, still pedalling but numb from head to tyre. The cliffs had a ticket booth. They wanted to charge people to go up and see the very tops of them. There must have been something up there if they were charging people to see it. Something good. I braked at the ticket booth and the brakes squealed. They needed lubricating oil. Maybe brand new brake pads. A man in a woolly jumper was nestled up inside with a flask and a crackling radio. His Jaffa cakes were up on a shelf beside him. I wanted one. I was starving.

'What are those cliffs?' I asked.

'They're the White Cliffs of Dover, son,' he said. He gave me a good looking over. 'You can't take that up though,' he said. 'You'll have to walk.'

'It's classed as a bicycle.'

'Doesn't matter if it's classed as a hovercraft, son. You can't take it up.'

I reached back and rooted out my plastic bag underneath the backseat. The cops hadn't found it. It still had notes inside. I squashed some under the glass. Little Queens stared up at the attendant with crumpled faces.

'Buy the missus something nice,' I said. I didn't know how much it was but I knew enough to know it was a lot.

'This real?' he said, and started to count it, arranging the heads in one bundle.

'There's nearly a hundred pounds here, son.'

'Can I have your Jaffa cakes?'

'You're not going up there to throw yourself off are you, son?'

'No, I'm not.'

'You don't look the best.'

'I'm fine. Just hungry.'

He slid two cans of tuna, a packet of crackers and the box of Jaffa cakes under

the plexiglass and waved me through.

'Do you have a can opener for the tuna?' I asked him.

'They're ring-pull.'

I cycled on.

The path to the top of the cliffs had no jagged edges. The rocks had been polished and smoothed out by the shoes that had climbed to the top before me to look at the nowhere else that there was to go. The hill was good and steep. I dug deep. A storm was moving in from France and winds warned me back off the edge.

I braked and ate the tuna like a wretched animal, drinking back the brine and mashing in the crackers and the Jaffa cakes all at once.

There were a couple of walkers kitted out in rainwear and hiking boots, walking past, giving me looks. Their eyebrows were down, scrutinizing me, not really knowing whether to laugh about me or call the cops. One thing was certain, they did not want a lift. Nobody would want a lift. With no possibility of fares, I felt lonely and useless.

I thought about going back to London.

The phone buzzed.

I stepped off the rickshaw, got it out from underneath the backseat and answered it.

'Hello.'

'Jesus Christ, Joe. Why the fuck have you not answered? Where have you been? Where are you? *He's here. He's answered.*'

'Hi Sis.'

'Where are you?'

'On some cliffs.'

'A policeman called. Said you were in jail.'

'I busted out.'

'This is what *he* did, you know that, don't you? This is exactly what he used to do—have everybody worrying to death about him.'

'Maybe he was trying to show us the way we shouldn't take, you know? Flying close to the sun to take our place, you know?'

'What? Are you all right? Where are you?'

'On some cliffs.'

'Jesus Christ. Look, just tell me where you are. I'll come get you.'

'No. Don't say that. Don't say that. I have to go. I'm sorry for making you worry. And I'm not drinking. I cycle now.'

'You're an alcoholic. The very same as Dad, the very same as him.'

The winds raged and the waves crashed in at the bottom of the cliffs like bombs. The walkers were gone and I was alone with the storm. 'And what if it has a point?'

'What?'

'What if they look back and it's not the scientists but the alcoholics and the junkies? What if they say that it was the dipsomaniacs and fiends that forged the path?'

'What path? What are you saying? I'll come get you.'

'Stop saying that. I've got to go,' I said, and hung up.

When I turned back the rickshaw was rolling towards the cliff edge.

I dived and slid along the wet grass headfirst, gaining on it in the slide, catching the back frame just as the front wheel slumped over the edge. The weight killed my arm. It started to drag me with it. I grabbed the back left wheel with my left, still holding the frame with my right and dug my toes into the earth, bringing it to a stop. Every muscle in my back and thighs was at full flex trying to pull it back to solid ground. I imagined it going over and smashing into the rocks as it plummeted, the plasterboard breaking first into a thousand pieces, a wheel snapping off, then another, nuts and bolts and rivets exploding from it and the whole thing finally crashing into the frothy rock and seaweed below. I got the front wheel back and upright on solid ground. I stood up and remounted right away, giving it a pedal to make sure it was all in working order then I cycled on, stopping for nothing or nobody.

RICKSHAWBOY

I told customs I was doing it for charity—Paris and
back in forty-eight hours. I rode west, along the
northern coast of France. It smelled like mussels and
salt. I wound through fields full of sugar beet, maize
and potatoes.

Pedalling took me down into a town and then
there was always an uphill out. It was uphill I pre-
ferred. There were no crowds, no mass theatre exo-
duses, no lost—only pinecones and cows so I wanted
16% inclines in twenty-five degree heat to compen-
sate. I wanted sweat-inducing steepness, every pedal
a struggle, fighting for every quarter of a rotation;
getting to the top and cycling on, hoping the next
uphill would be 19% so I could fight that too, roar
at it, fistfight it if I could, pummel and rage into its
weakness against me.

My knees, shoulders, lips and hands all got badly
sunburnt. My skin peeled after a few days. The paint
on the crossbar cracked too, and the skin and the
paint sailed off into the countryside on the breezes.
Gravel caked the inside of the front brake pads. My

brain was sun-drenched and I was seeing spots and rainbows. The chainset and the derailleur clogged with more gravel. The rickshaw slowed. My feet had fungus, the pedals were loosening and both cranks felt brittle. My shins splinted and the nuts and bolts squeaked and the back brakes eventually bubbled inside, becoming unresponsive. The leather had torn on the saddle and I had to push my palms down hard on the handlebars to relieve the pinching from its metal. The gears all wore into one. The chain went unoiled and it slipped constantly, and when it did, my right knee would slam against the steering column.

My body was pumping so much blood that a twinge had started in my heart. It turned into a crunching pain and worsened every time I took the gulping breaths I needed to stay going. The pain coiled itself around my heart and then spread stinging tentacles across my chest and underneath my left shoulder. There were flushes and dizzy head rushes. The heart was telling me to stop, that I was a dying thing. I told it we were all dying things and bought energy drinks in local *magasins* but they made it worse. The pain seared. I both loved and hated it. It was the only thing I was absolutely certain about. At night time, acid would seize my whole body stiff and I would lay in the backseat in palpitations, having lucid dreams of handless riders and newly born tricycles, the heart beating as loud as a war drum, waiting for death to arrive when my body finally said enough was enough.

One morning I woke after the night's wind had frozen me through. The sun was out and acting like nothing had happened. The sky was completely blue and a small boy in shorts stood beside me, a coffee in his hand that he put down beside me.

'Merci,' I said.

He ran back through the fence into his family-owned campsite and stood by his mother. She was looking at me strangely, trying to figure it out until couples and families arrived to the breakfast area wanting orange juice, coffee and croissants before hitting the road with their campervans and touring bicycles. A group of ten guys came to the outside veranda for breakfast in last nights clothes, pulled three tables together and packed around them with sick heads and red eyes, defeated in hangovers and content to sit through the throb while nursing a coffee and pinching off stamp-sized bits of croissant. One of the guys who wore sunglasses, refused the coffee and ordered a beer. The little boy's mother was nervous. *Really*, she seemed to ask. *It's morning.*

Yes, the guy said, *a beer.*

She got him one. He sat with it, staring into its bubbles, into the casino-amber. He took off his sunglasses and stared harder, his eyes like punched rhubarb with a cut across the bridge of the nose. He looked lost, like a poet searching for a first line. He drank the beer back in one and ordered another. And then another.

After the three breakfast beers he looked around at the other nine guys and rasped. He moved his chair over to face a pot-plant and began a conversation, making sure the others realised that it was because the pot-plant was more fun than them. He went to the outside fridge and got himself another beer to be put down on the bill. The woman threw her hands up in the air at the ignorance of it. The guy started to play table tennis by himself, with no ball or paddle, running from one side of the table to the other, hitting imaginary shots so as to return the imaginary ball to himself. Eventually he won and roared victoriously. The woman saw trouble ahead and called her husband who stopped watering the gardens and hovered around the veranda. The husband asked him to keep it down and the guy exaggerated being extra quiet, walking around on his tiptoes with a finger over his lips. He sank the rest of the beer and dropped the bottle on the tile accidently. It smashed. The woman got pissed off and angry with her husband. The guy apologised and tried to get the brush and pan from the kitchen to clean it up. The husband asked him to sit down, that he would do it, just please, sit down. The guy took offense and went for another beer in the fridge. The woman refused to give it to him. The husband stood in his way and asked him to leave the veranda. The guy shouted insults. The nine others told him to ease up, that it was breakfast for God's sake and he was being a complete dickhead. The guy told the whole lot of them to go fuck themselves.

It was then he saw me on the rickshaw and came on through the fence and into the car-park.

'Bonjour,' he said.

'Hello,' I said. 'Bonjour.'

'*I want to go home*,' he said loudly so the campsite behind him would hear.

'Where do you live?'

The guy had been joking I think but saw that I was serious and so got serious in return.

'I live in Deauville,' he said. 'It's far. After Le Havre.'

'West?'

'Oui.'

'I was going that way anyway. Hop on.'

'Vraiment?'

'Yes, vraiment. Come on,' I said. He ran back into the campsite to retrieve a bag while I knocked back the rest of my coffee.

'Je m'appelle Maurice,' he said on his return.

'Je m'appelle Irish.'

Maurice stood up on the backseat, balancing like a surfer, shouting farewell to all the campsite bastards. He was a big guy and it was a while since there was a person on the backseat. My chest felt his weight and the heart strained. My stomach tightened and I had to pull the handlebars hard from my shoulders. His friends were glad to see him go and none of them asked him to stop, to come back.

There were squashed birds on the road, two dimensional except for a wing or a foot that sprung out into the universe, yet to be trampled by a tyre, and CD's, lots of them, one a kilometre, drivers having had enough of the same songs over and over.

The campervans rolled past, in no rush, dogs hanging out the passenger windows to enjoy the morning air. Maurice barked at one. The dog did not know what to say. Maurice howled to bait the dog but the dog looked like he had seen his fair share of things and we were nothing special. Housewives waited for the breadman by the pleached hedges of their front gates. The sea arrived at our right and then it disappeared as the road climbed into the hinterland then rolled back down into another cove with a town tucked inside. The road kept coming and Maurice was still standing, waiting for something, that first line almost arriving but not quite.

'I think I would like wine,' he said.

We stopped at the next *magasin*. He ran in and got two bottles. I kept a backwards pedal so as to keep moving.

'Do you know Freddie Mercury, Irish?' he asked when we were back on the road and he had downed some wine.

'I do,' I said.

'Is this the real life?' he asked.

The people in the cars and campervans went about their journey, reading novels and magazines, tending babies, drawing designs in condensation and swabbing it clean again, rubbing the back of a partner's neck, sorting through photos on a camera or musing on a text from a friend in another place, travelling in another direction. Cyclists passed us, no backseats attached.

Maurice sang and drank.

Forgotten days and nights, arguments, fights and public scenes, rock bottoms and disgraceful carry-on passed us by. Being hired and fired, quitting in a storming rage, changing address, bad tattoos, wasted weeks, ex-friends, failed relationships and little fluttering regret bats all zoomed past with the Normandy countryside.

'Sends shivers down my spine, body's aching all the time,' Maurice sang and stood up for the solo, playing air-guitar right in the face of a whirlwind roar of Octobers and Thursdays, dizzy Junes, off-days and Monday mornings, dawns and deadlines, Birthdays, work-training days: the clock going back an hour, forward an hour, back an hour. We took lefts, rights and went straight ahead, turned and veered, speed bumps and cats eyes thumping underwheel. I pedalled and Maurice drank more wine. We both carried on with *Bohemian Rhapsody*.

Chat, talks and conversations flew past us, about the happy moments and what makes it all worthwhile, about problems with the marriage and packing it all in; chat about maybe-it-would-be-better-if-I-was-gone, chat that eased grudges and moulded new ones, chat that was forgotten as soon as it was spoken and chat that was replayed in your mind for years afterwards.

A car slowed to our side to take a photograph of us because we looked so mental. I caught my reflection in its window. I had not seen myself in a long time. I was haggard. My brow had big creases and my face was old. And then I realised it was not my reflection at all but my father sitting in the backseat of a Peugeot staring back at me. He noticed me, too and we stared at one another sceptically, both of us knowing the uncanniness of the situation. I told him to wind down the window with a handle gesture but he just stared. The Peugeot sped away.

The campervans were all turning off the road and making for new campsites. We rolled into Le Harve and kept going, through the city in the late evening. We came to the port. Lorries were parked up for the night with the drivers inside the cabins snoozing. Signs for the Pont du Normandie Bridge started to show on the roadside.

For no other option available, I took the motor-way, the speed limit getting notched up to 110 kilo-metres an hour, trucks whizzing by ferociously, driv-ers reaching for their phones to grab a picture of the two nutcases on the motorway with a rickshaw. There were no longer squashed birds or CDs. Instead, there was broken mirror, glass, bolts, nuts and bits of dash-board. Animals did not die there, cars and trucks did. Maurice was a little scared but he saw I was not stop-ping, and accepted his fate, whatever it was.

The Pont du Normandie was a monstrosity, a steep and winding feat of engineering held together by a cobweb of cables that brought the motorway across the mouth of the Seine. I dug deep. Maurice sang and I joined in when I could. The wind was so strong that when I spat it dissolved into the air and spun about in a million bits of spray. There were oil refineries and gravel pits below us the size of golf balls. We reached the top and began to freewheel down the other side, through a tollbooth with an attendant looking at us with her mouth wide open.

The evening was late when we rolled into Deauville. I braked down by the harbour. There were long crocodile-shaped rocks dappling in the tide and the sun was still hot even in its set, the air warm and the evening not so bad, a nice place to pass out. Maurice had snoozed off in the backseat. I fell off the saddle into a pile of fishing nets, turning to face the sun, smothered by pain in every part of my body. My legs twitched and I could not get them to stop.

Shadows hung from everything like backseats, rooting things down, inescapable in the light. Inescapable in the sun. As long as there was sun, I thought, there would be shadows. It felt like the most profound thing ever attempted by a thinking person, so slender a concept that if it were to be worded it would be lost. I rolled it around in my head. Shadows and sun, sun and shadows. I wondered how it had gone unpondered by mankind up until that moment, around for millennia of human consciousness but never realised.

One of the shadows moved towards us. It was like a thick soup suspended mid-air. It came closer—a swarm of midges, feeding on the last of the sun's rays, the evening probably the end for most of them. The midges moved in on us and beat against our faces.

Maurice woke.

'Deauville,' I said. 'You're home.'

His eyes had swelled and they were truly black now. The cut on the bridge of his nose had crusted over with a black-red scab. He staggered off the back-seat, stood up on the harbour wall, unbuckled his belt, tore open his fly and directed his stream of piss out to sea amidst the millions of midges on their last legs.

ANDY

There was a crunch and the pedals locked. I stood up and pressed hard to force them on. There was a snap, the pedals went limp and I slammed into the steering column, my knee taking yet another battering.

I feared a snapped chain with all my tired heart.

I looked underneath and sure enough, there it drooped from the chainset like a shot snake—coiled and dead. I tried to cycle on, to see if by some miracle a rickshaw would work without a chain. It did not. There was nothing around—no garage, no bike repair shops and I did not have a spare link or calipers to fix it.

I lugged the bastard on by the handlebars.

On the uphills I had to go behind them and push. The backend would roll over an ankle if I left one dragging for too long and the weight would trap my foot. It took all my strength to lift it off and the foot came back bloody, bruised and grazed. I finally devised a harness using the chain as a set of reigns. I wrapped it around the handlebars, held it at my shoulders and pulled. The horses in the fields had a right laugh.

I thought he was a soldier at first, standing there on the side of the road in a military green t-shirt and camouflage combats. He was about seventy years old. He wore a baseball cap, *Florida* on the front. He had been white starting out in life but now he was a deep tanned brown, like varnished toffee.

'God damn it,' he shouted, looking down the road then up the road then down the road again. 'God damn it, God damn it, God damn it.'

He spotted me and waited where he was standing, trying to act casual as the sunburnt fiend pulling a rickshaw by its chain through Normandy approached. I think he was pawning off the weirdness as just another cultural difference for him. It could have been a *thing* in France for all he knew so he didn't mention it.

'Hey kid, you know where Omaha Beach is at around here?' he said, changing the way he spoke for nobody, not even if they didn't speak English.

'You're about eighty years too late.'

'Well smack my ass—someone talks American. Where you from?'

'I'm Irish.'

'I'm Irish, too,' he said. 'My great grandmother was from County Sligo.'

The Americans jumped on the Irish bandwagon and I was in no mood to talk about how beautiful Sligo was and his great grandmother's surname.

'You're more than likely of German origin, statistically speaking.'

'First guy I talk to in a week and I want to punch him in his goddamn face,' he said. 'I'm Andy.'

'I'm Irish,' I said, and we shook hands.

'Irish your name too, huh? That's easy. You don't look so good. What's the matter with your chariot?'

'Chain broke.'

'This chain?' he asked, taking it away from me. He lifted up his t-shirt and there was a utility belt tied around his waist. There was a mini-hammer, a Swiss-army knife, screwdrivers, a GPS device, a canister of pepper spray, a bottle of water, a torch doubling as a baton, a camera and other pouches and zippers for things I could not see.

Andy took hold of the rickshaw and lifted it on its side. He threaded the dead chain back through and around, caught it by both ends then reached inside a pouch.

'It's a link for a motorcycle chain I got but this chain here doesn't look like your average bicycle chain. I don't understand these goddamn European measurements. Millilitres or some such shit, goddamn it.'

He took out a pair of pliers and snapped the link on. The chain was fixed.

'You need oil on this,' Andy said, taking out a mini-bottle of oil and ran the nozzle over the chain. 'You're all good.'

I had no words.

'Well, you gonna take me to Omaha Beach on this or what?'

Andy hopped on and put his two arms out straight across the backseat. I cycled on.

'I thought you were a soldier,' I said over my shoulder.

'I was in Korea. That was enough for me. Christ.'

'So why do you still dress like a soldier?'

'Why are you on a chariot?'

'It's a rickshaw. Chariots have horses.'

'Rickshaw then. You little son of a bitch,' he said. 'You need to get laid, kid. I got two girls. One for the road and one for everyday. Then I got a goddamn ex-wife who's looking to reconcile. All back in the States.'

'One for the road?'

'I take motorcycle trips. The everyday girl's got a kid, doesn't like being on the road much anyhow. Two of 'em hate one other but what you gonna do?'

'Where's your motorcycle now?'

'I rented a car, figured I could sleep in it, too, save some money on these hotels they got here. I just can't remember where I left the little piece of shit. I'd leave it but they got my credit card. Wouldn't care much if they charged its *worth* to the card—six bucks or some such shit. I got more horse power up my ass.'

Signs for the American Cemetery and Memorial as well as Omaha Beach started to pop up on the road. We rolled into the small town of Colleville-sur-mer. American flags hung from the houses. Plaques and tributes and photographs of American soldiers were all around. The liberators they were called.

'I think I've been in this goddamn town,' said Andy, looking around. 'Parked my car somewhere around here. That guy—'

Andy was pointing to a Frenchman sitting outside a café smoking a Gauloises. 'Told me to walk the whole goddamn other direction, goddamn it. Hey! You told me the whole other goddamn direction.'

The Frenchman shrugged.

'Guy's an asshole,' Andy said.

The hedges became as neat as a haircut. We followed a road down to the front gates of the American Cemetery and Memorial. There were coaches and mini-vans of tourists, mainly American. I brought Andy as far as they allowed cars and bicycles and braked.

'You not coming in?' he asked.

'No.'

'Come in you stupid son-of-a-bitch or I'll take my chain link back.'

'I don't want to leave the rickshaw.'

'You married to the goddamn thing?'

'Yeah, sort of.'

'Well, she'll be OK for forty-five minutes. Christ.'

'I can't leave it.'

'Well ride it in then.'

'I don't think they allow rickshaws.'

'I allow rickshaws. Now ride it in.'

A group of Yanks passed in their white trainers and golf visors looking at us.

'I'm doing this with an Irish guy who looks like he has the bubonic plague,' Andy said to them. 'I want my fuckin' head checked I tell ya. Married to his goddamn chariot.'

They smiled awkwardly and picked up the pace.

I cycled through the reception centre and we got attention from the security guys immediately. Andy told them all to beat it—told them they were douche-bags—told them he didn't take shrapnel in his knee in Kaesong for a pair of snot-nose sons-of-bitches to not allow chariots into his country's cemetery.

'Rules are rules, sir,' one said.

'You stare down an M-16 and talk to me about rules,' shouted Andy. 'Now pedal this goddamn chariot inside, kid.'

The security guys backed off.

We went straight out into the lawns. Brilliant white crosses and stars of David stretched out as far as we could see on perfect green grass.

'We missed all our bombs,' Andy said. 'English hit their targets at least. But when we came, the Germans were firing down on us like the goddamn fires of Hell. Here were guys trying to defeat evil and restore freedom. And not the goddamn freedom in the douchebag way we use it now. *Real* freedom: the freedom of a continent. Here was a generation with a purpose. What we got today, huh?'

We sat looking at the 9,000 white tombstones. Soldiers, sailors and airmen. 9,000 guys who never got home.

Andy got off the backseat and took a walk by himself.

The nearest cross to me belonged to a Private Sean Fitzgerald killed in action on the 6th of June 1944. 18 years old. The beach below was Omaha, a long way down to the water, a long way soldiers had had to run from the boat to safety, machine guns loaded and ready.

Fitzgerald. It was my name, too. I hadn't thought of it in a while.

'Hello, son,' said my father, having arrived home with a new cut across his forehead.

'No milk?' I asked.

'No, didn't get 'round to getting the milk.'

'Where's the car?'

'In a ditch,' he said, taking the keys out of his pocket and placing them on the kitchen table. 'You can try get it out if you want.'

He needed upset and disappointment and tears. I knew this. But sometimes it was impossible not to rise to him.

'Jesus Christ,' I shouted. 'You're the dumbest man I know. Everyone's just starting to get back on track and you start drinking again.'

'My blood is in your veins,' he said. 'Remember that.'

'I'm nothing like you.'

He smiled like I knew nothing and he knew everything, took a bottle of whiskey from under his coat and drank from it.

'Nothing like you,' I repeated.

He let his breath out loud and dramatic after the drink. He wiped his mouth. I grabbed the bottle from him and poured it down the kitchen sink.

'We'll see, son,' he said, and walked out the back door again to go and replace the whiskey.

I could feel flowers in the wreaths overtaking. I could feel the grass beneath the wheels zooming on by. I could feel the statues lapping me. It was like I was one of those professional queue-folk back in the West End who spent life in a line, waiting. I tried to make sense of things, reasoning it all out, practicing not just what I wanted to say but the tone of how I said it, replacing words for other words, coming at the argument from different angles, getting angry, getting sad, drifting in and out of stupor, aching, worrying, wanting to cycle on but having to wait.

'Hello, son,' said a voice at last. He was looking at the cross. I knew he had been there for some time but the silence had been thick and impossible to cut. *Hello, son.* I had to hand it to him—it was good.

'Hello, Dad.'

'Fitzgerald.'

'Coincidence all right,' I said.

'Some bicycle you have there.'

'They call it a rickshaw. Well, pedicab or bike-taxi, really. The Yank I'm with calls it a chariot.'

'Where are you coming from with it?'

'London.'

'Fair aul cycle. You couldn't have got yourself a car?'

'Lost my license.'

'Mr. Perfect lost his license, did he? Isn't that something? Drink?'

'The apple never falls too far,' I said.

'Well, well, well. Mr. Perfect lost his license for drink. I remember Mr. Perfect giving me a big high and mighty speech about losing my license once. Alcoholic—that's all I ever heard from you, son. You're not much better. Look at you, how long's it been since you've not been on this thing? This rickshaw. Sorry, bike-taxi.'

'I can bring you home on it,' I said.

'Bit late for that,' he said.

'I thought it could put an end to things.'

'An end?'

'Yes.'

'To what things?'

'Well, I never went to your funeral as you probably noticed. So, I never really got closure.'

As soon as I said it I regretted it. He laughed. I knew he would. Because I had used the word, *closure.* A word like closure had no place in a conversation with my father. Closure was for cry-baby Americans on the television.

'Closure, eh?'

'I just thought I could give you a lift home, that's all.'

'Well, it's too late.'

'When you called me to come get you that night I was angry. And tired.'

'Closure,' he repeated with a cynical bite attached.

'I just thought it would bring it to an end that's all. I'm tired. I'm so tired.'

'Closure—that's a good one.'

'Well, great talking you again, Dad.'

'Sorry your little symbolic gesture for closure didn't work out. On you go, on your little bike-taxi,' he sneered and walked away down through the crosses.

It had been a stalemate. A no-fare. A fail. I took the rejection, word for word, and stole away with it, rolling it over and over again in my head.

'Don't mention closure,' I said. 'Or losing the license.'

The waves crashed down on Omaha Beach and the wind upped a gear. I backpedalled to keep moving, pedalling and pedalling on the spot, going absolutely nowhere but back and back into time until I was in Ballybailte, by the door of Phelans, which looked like it had changed ownership. The new coat of paint was a dead giveaway. Publicans could give it ten years before they had to give it up, for the health or for the sake of the marriage. A new publican would buy it, give it a lick of paint and start pouring pints. Sometimes they changed the name. This guy had not. It was still Phelans. The flags were out for the football. The team must have had a final coming up.

The bargirl came out a side door. She said hello. I said hello back. Her boyfriend collected by her in his Subaru Legacy with blacked out back windows. He was a few years older than her. It was always the way. The couple motored off for a quick ride in the backseat before he dropped her home then the town fell dead quiet as it must have been on the night he died.

'Hello, son,' he said again from the front door of Phelans.

'Hello, Dad.'

'Some bicycle you have there.'

'Thanks.'

'Where are you coming from with it?'

'Just around. Stopped by to see if you might want a lift anywhere?'

'I'm grand where I am, thanks.'

'You sure? I'm going your way anyway.'

'I seem to remember asking you for a lift once, son. What was it you said?'

'I was angry.'

'What was it you said, though? Oh that's right. Walk you said. Run down by a
car I was—lying there in a ditch, dying alone.'

'You were a good man, Dad. I know you were. You weren't like this. This is all I have of you though. Please, take the lift. I tried not to be like you. I tried to do things different but I think I ended up the very same.'

'My blood is in your veins,' he said and walked away.

I called myself a cretin, told myself to just fuck-off, backpedalled until my quads seized, spots and rainbows, everything on the tip of my tongue, reality and madness getting mashed up in the clicking chain, all the same to me, all meaning the same, pedalling back on into the past, time travel of sorts, trying to reason it out, justify it, getting angry with it, telling him he was the stupidest man I know, trying to always get the last word with him, telling him I loved him, a neverending battle to get to the very crux of it.

'Hello, son.'

'Hello, Dad. Ever been on a rickshaw before?'

'I haven't.'

'You never forget your first. Don't worry Dad, haven't crashed in hours. Get you there in no time. Hop on. Gets you to the liquor quicker, you like that one? I'll take you home. No charge. I'll take you home. Hop on, quickly now before the curtain-up, we've only got four minutes.'

'There's no way I'm taking a lift on that,' he said. 'That thing has no insurance I'll wager. Are they even legal? What about safety? Crash that thing at 30 miles per hour and I'd say you wouldn't walk away from it.'

'Don't worry, they're safe, Dad. Hop on.'

'It'll be a cold day in Hell before I go with you on that,' he said and walked away.

I started to cry.

'Kid,' Andy said, snapping me out of it. 'I've been around some crazy motherfuckers in my life but—who were you talking to?'

'Myself,' I said.

Andy thought about it for a while. 'They got shrinks in France?'

I wanted to tell him that I was tired, and my heart was hurting me, and I needed help but I did not know how to say it to him. It seemed insignificant anyway standing there in a field with 9,000 heroes. Not far away was La Cambe, the German cemetery with 21,000 men who never got home in that one. We sat for the longest time listening to the waves, saying nothing, not mentioning the other's tears because we were men. The cemetery was all so beautiful and horrifically tragic at the same time, a giant oxymoron of a thing to figure out. One guy in Germany back in 1945 wanting to go one direction with things, everyone else wanting to go another. After a while, Andy wiped his face with the palm of his hand and I wiped mine.

The past was to be learned from. It was there to make the future better, there so that we could all have it better.

'So, where you going again on that rickshaw thing of yours?'

'I'm going home,' I said. 'I'm getting tired.'

'Home, huh? Ireland?'

'Yeah. Come on. We'll get a cup of coffee back at the café.'

'Kid—whatever about chariots on the lawns here but they ain't having you in the goddamn café on it.'

'I'll leave it outside.'

'You buyin'?'

'Yeah, I'm buying you cheap bastard,' I said, and helped him up.

THE FERRY HOME

Shouts went out about the all clear. The ferry doors closed. Turbines powered-up, slow at first like they were trying to cut through washing-up liquid.

There was a fight once, back in London when I was in the thick of pedalling. I came across it because I had taken a couple to Stoke Newington in the early hours of the morning. I was pedalling back to the West End through a residential area when I came across two fighting men, one naked, one wearing clothes.

'Now,' the man wearing clothes said to the naked man who he had pinned to the ground. 'What you going to do now? Fuck my wife? That what you going to do? Beat me up and fuck my wife?'

The naked man kicked upwards, stood fast with his teeth grit and launched an attack of his own, throwing windmill punches, landing half but getting thrown off balance by his misses.

'Lads,' I said. 'Take it easy.'

They ignored me and the clothed man got the naked man in a headlock.

I thought about intervening, about getting off the rickshaw and coming between them but from behind me, a woman in bare feet with big, black curly hair came bounding down the street, her breasts popping out of her halter-top as she ran. When she reached the men she used her palm to hit the clothed man across the ear and face.

'Let him go,' she screamed. 'Let him go.'

'I've had enough of this shit,' the naked man said and spat a wad of blood then stomped off, his penis flouncing about like a child throwing a tantrum at being dragged from a birthday party.

The clothed man saw that the woman's breasts were on display and pulled up her halter-top to cover them. He took her by the wrist and led her back to where she came from. 'One more, Liz,' he said. 'One more and I swear to God.'

The naked man stood at the top of the road for a second like an eyeballed city fox then jumped a wall and disappeared.

I felt alone.

And just then a hotdog vendor appeared with his dingy cart, on his way home for the night.

I always admired the hotdog vendors. They would set up on a street corner with their carts and a bag of buns and hotdogs, selling it all to the post-pub crowd at two pounds a pop—tomato sauce provided. Onions for an extra fifty pence. Inevitably, every single night, at least once, cops would ask them for their vendor license which none of them possessed. They would get the food safety act cited to them and then would be marched to the nearest rubbish bin and forced to throw out their illegal food. The hotdog vendors would walk back to their base to restock and be selling hotdogs again twenty minutes later. It was a lesson in resilience—guys who went out knowing their future each night and went on regardless.

The vendor stopped beside me, opened up his cart and asked, 'You like onions?'

'Not really,' I said.

He handed me a hotdog. 'No onions,' he said.

'Thanks,' I said. 'I appreciate it. Thank you.'

'It's only a hotdog,' he said, and walked on.

'It's only a hotdog,' I said as the ferry embarked from Cherbourg. I looked at my rickshaw still on the port. 'It's only a hotdog.'

The rickshaw became as small as a tricycle then it was a black dot then it disappeared and all there was to see was snot-green sea at dusk so I went inside.

At first there was gentle swaying but soon, when we were out in the thick of sea and weather, the swell became more severe. My head ached. I felt sick and there were sixteen hours remaining. I found a hall-way without any passengers in it and lay down on the floor. The lights went out, the swell in the channel worsened, the ferry creaked and the pitch black filled up with petrol fumes. Irish folk songs from the bar seeped through the walls—*And I spent all my money on whiskey and beer.*

I began to have God-awful visions of a rickshaw-less world, capsized in the depths with nowhere to pedal. My legs started spinning in small circles. Waves crashed against the hull, their splash washing across the top decks, the salt fizzing against the steel.

I started to count.

*A haon, a do, a tri, a ceathair, a haon, a do, a tri, a ceathair, a haon a do, a tri, a ceathair...*waiting in the dark, curled up and trapped, counting and pedalling air. *A haon, a do, a tri, a ceathair...*

Alone in the dark with my hurting heart I felt like the old guys who still rented a rickshaw but never used it. They had once been wild, rickshawing everywhere in London, any fare, anywhere. Then they found a lucky spot and stayed there more and more until that was the only place they would stay, waiting for fares to come to them, not bothering with the hunt for fares anymore, it all too much trouble. Then they did not take the rickshaw out during the week. They stayed in the base and played cards on their backseats. They only pedalled at the weekends when it was busy enough. And then they skipped weekends. They just paid rent or bought the rickshaw outright, and spent the time sitting on it back at the base with bad hearts and stories of when.

A haon, a do, a tri, a ceathair...

Another night, there was a little man in a tuxedo who had his head in the lap of his tall, blonde and beautiful wife in the backseat. I had to take them to

257

the Ritz in Green Park. The man was crying and his wife was petting him across the forehead.

'Shush. Shush now, my poor little baby,' she said.

'I just can't take it. You know I can't take it. The way he looks at you. And flirts with you. I love you so fucking much. Do you know that?'

'I love you, too. Excuse me driver but we seem to be going around in circles.'

'Sorry about that—same price. There's just a few diversions,' I said, needing the fare to keep me going until the pub-closing rush at 12:30.

'But *do* you know? How much I really love you?'

'I know my little baby. I love you, too. Excuse me driver, but we really seem to be going around in circles. What diversions?'

Sometimes the whole city seemed to be in turmoil. Like once, when a brawl spilled out from a club on Leicester Square—thirty guys up in each other's faces and nobody backing down. The hotheads threw the first punches. The knocked-down guys got back up, came around the side of the fracas with punches from blind spots. The girlfriends got in the faces of the other side, telling them to fuck right off while their boyfriends were being held back, crying *stab me then tough guy, come on, stab me.* A girlfriend got a punch in the chin and the whole thing turned mushroom cloud, fights and tussles, kicks to the head. The girlfriends cried and their mascara ran. The man in the dress showed up and started saying, 'I don't believe this. All in the limo havin' a laugh and they throw this dress on me.' Then there was glass, and someone had taken out a knife. The undercovers had exploded from the mobile processing unit but made a difference to nothing. The sirens arrived and their light turned it all blue. Some of the girlfriends pointed to where the stabber had supposedly run off towards but the cops were looking up at the CCTV cameras, waiting to hear back from control as to who were the main perpetrators but a lot of the perpetrators needed ambulances and a lot of the original victims were now hightailing perpetrators.

An undercover sat on a wall looking thoughtful. He had a bloody mouth and a ripped t-shirt. I admired him, having tried to stop conflict, thinking he could, thinking he was nearly there, if he could just reach that tiny bit further to catch it.

'All right?' Marie said on opening the door. She looked beautiful if a bit afraid, like she thought she was about to be taken hostage.

'All right,' I said. 'Sorry for just showing up. I didn't have your number or anything to see if it was OK.'

'You've lost weight,' said Vanessa from behind her in the doorway.

'Yeah,' I said.

'Are you still drinking?' Vanessa barged on.

'No,' I said. 'I don't drink anymore. Been doing a lot of cycling.'

'Where?' Vanessa asked.

'I was in London for a while.'

'Loads a'mad yokes over there I'd say, are there?'

'Yeah.'

'Is that your sister in the car?'

'Yeah, that's Niamh.'

'Does she want to come in?'

'She's going shopping. I said I'd come up with her and call in to see how the ballet was going.'

'I gave it up,' Vanessa said.

'She was kicked out for hitting another girl,' Marie said.

'I do karate now,' Vanessa said.

'My niece does karate. She's your age. I think you'd like her.'

'Maybe,' Vanessa said. 'So, you just called up?'

'Yeah.'

'Do you fancy my Mam?'

I laughed. Vanessa laughed. Marie laughed.

'I was just dropping her down to karate actually,' Marie said. 'I'm walking her down. Would you like to walk with us?'

'Yeah,' I said. 'A walk sounds good.'